gd

Eric's longing astonished him

After all these years, he'd believed he was cured.
He hadn't even acknowledged until now that there
was anything to be cured of.

Anne was different from the other women he'd
known. He'd gotten lost in her sensuality and her
unrestrained eagerness. She'd held nothing back
from him.

Thank goodness he'd come back to his cottage.
There was no chance of running into Anne tonight,
and by tomorrow he would have himself under
control.

Two sharp knocks startled him. It didn't matter
who it was; Eric would be grateful for anyone to
take his mind off the past.

"Come on in," he drawled, and then his heart
performed a couple of loop-the-loops.

There she stood, temptation itself. Anne. The
woman of his dreams. Not the one he had
promised to marry, but the one he ached to
take to his bed....

D1012076

ABOUT THE AUTHOR

Jacqueline Diamond had been a bridesmaid twice and a maid of honor once. She herself has been married for twenty years. The mother of two school-age sons, Jackie is a former Associated Press reporter. You can write to her at P.O. Box 1315, Brea, CA 92822.

Books by Jacqueline Diamond

HARLEQUIN AMERICAN ROMANCE

HARLEQUIN INTRIGUE

Don't miss any of our special offers. Write to us at the following address for information on our newest releases.

Harlequin Reader Service
U.S.: 3010 Walden Ave., P.O. Box 1325, Buffalo, NY 14269
Canadian: P.O. Box 609, Fort Erie, On t. L2A 5X3

Assignment: Groom!

JACQUELINE DIAMOND

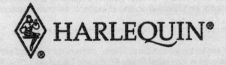

TORONTO • NEW YORK • LONDON
AMSTERDAM • PARIS • SYDNEY • HAMBURG
STOCKHOLM • ATHENS • TOKYO • MILAN • MADRID
PRAGUE • WARSAW • BUDAPEST • AUCKLAND

If you purchased this book without a cover you should be aware
that this book is stolen property. It was reported as "unsold and
destroyed" to the publisher, and neither the author nor the
publisher has received any payment for this "stripped book."

For Julie Kistler and Pamela Browning, who have
gone out of their way to be helpful!

ISBN 0-373-16791-1

ASSIGNMENT: GROOM!

Copyright © 1999 by Jackie Hyman.

All rights reserved. Except for use in any review, the reproduction or
utilization of this work in whole or in part in any form by any electronic,
mechanical or other means, now known or hereafter invented, including
xerography, photocopying and recording, or in any information storage
or retrieval system, is forbidden without the written permission of the
publisher, Harlequin Enterprises Limited, 225 Duncan Mill Road,
Don Mills, Ontario, Canada M3B 3K9.

All characters in this book have no existence outside the imagination of
the author and have no relation whatsoever to anyone bearing the same
name or names. They are not even distantly inspired by any individual
known or unknown to the author, and all incidents are pure invention.

This edition published by arrangement with Harlequin Books S.A.

® and TM are trademarks of the publisher. Trademarks indicated with
® are registered in the United States Patent and Trademark Office, the
Canadian Trade Marks Office and in other countries.

Visit us at www.romance.net

Printed in U.S.A.

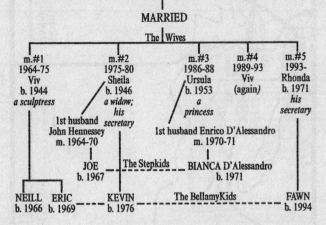

WILLIAM "BUDGE" BELLAMY aka The Pretzel King b. 1939

MARRIED

The Wives

m.#1
1964-75
Viv
b. 1944
a sculptress

m.#2
1975-80
Sheila
b. 1946
a widow;
his
secretary

m.#3
1986-88
Ursula
b. 1953
a
princess

m.#4
1989-93
Viv
(again)

m.#5
1993-
Rhonda
b. 1971
his
secretary

1st husband
John Hennessey
m. 1964-70

1st husband Enrico D'Alessandro
m. 1970-71

JOE
b. 1967

The Stepkids

BIANCA D'Alessandro
b. 1971

NEILL
b. 1966

ERIC
b. 1969

KEVIN
b. 1976

The Bellamy Kids

FAWN
b. 1994

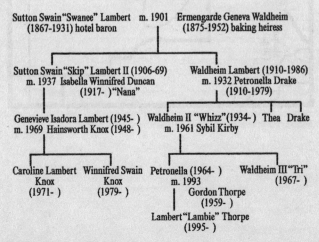

Lambert Family Tree

Sutton Swain "Swanee" Lambert
(1867-1931) hotel baron

m. 1901

Ermengarde Geneva Waldheim
(1875-1952) baking heiress

Sutton Swain "Skip" Lambert II (1906-69)
m. 1937 Isabella Winnifred Duncan
(1917-) "Nana"

Waldheim Lambert (1910-1986)
m. 1932 Petronella Drake
(1910-1979)

Genevieve Isadora Lambert (1945-)
m. 1969 Hainsworth Knox (1948-)

Waldheim II "Whizz" (1934-)
m. 1961 Sybil Kirby

Thea Drake

Caroline Lambert
Knox
(1971-)

Winnifred Swain
Knox
(1979-)

Petronella (1964-)
m. 1993
Gordon Thorpe
(1959-)

Waldheim III "Tri"
(1967-)

Lambert "Lambie" Thorpe
(1995-)

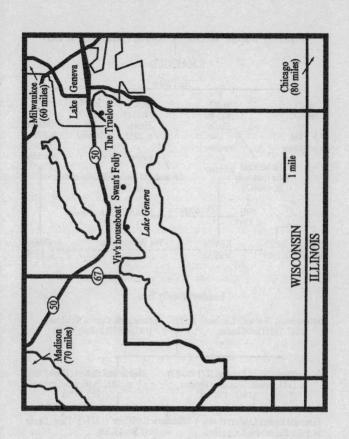

Prologue

Anne Crumm couldn't believe she was waking up next to Eric Bellamy.

California sunshine filtered through the miniblinds, striping his muscular torso and his lean hips, which the rumpled covers bared almost to a critical point. Although his face was turned away, there was no mistaking the shape of his sculpted head and the dark, stylishly cut hair.

Or the distinctive scent, half animal magnetism and half sleek sophistication. Exactly what *had* happened between them?

Anne hadn't exactly blacked out last night, but, in her early morning stupor, the details remained fuzzy. Maybe she wasn't quite ready to grasp the full implications.

Around her studio apartment lay the remains of the previous evening's activities. They'd worked late on a last-minute assignment handed down by Laurie Furness, their editor at *CoolNotes* magazine. The deadline was noon today.

On the breakfast bar clustered two soda cans, a pizza box, two wineglasses and an almost empty bottle. The battered desk in the corner nearly vanished beneath her secondhand computer, his expensive laptop, her telephone, his cell phone, stacks of printouts and notes. They'd been enormously productive—both before and after they knocked off at 2:00 a.m.

Especially afterward. They had definitely done the deed, Anne reflected ruefully. She could no longer suppress the memory; in fact, she intended to cherish it.

Her senses hummed with the memory of their lovemaking. She could feel herself coming awake, everywhere.

Eric stirred sleepily on the foldout couch. "What time is it?"

"The clock's on your side." Anne was not given to indulging men, even when they resembled Greek gods and left her body with a residual glow.

He rolled toward the clock. "Ten? You're kidding!" Eric stretched his well-toned body and arched abruptly into a seated position. "Laurie's going to kill us!"

"Correction—Laurie's going to kill *me*," she said. "As for you, she might not genuflect quite as deeply as usual when you walk into the office."

His laugh startled her with its warmth. "You've got a wonderful way with words."

"Tell that to Laurie when we hand in our article. Of course, she'll be certain that you did all the work and I merely watched in girlish awe." Anne finger-combed her straight, light-brown hair so it fell in a curtain around her. She felt like a turtle, finding safety inside its shell.

"Don't sell yourself short. Why do you think she assigned us to work together?" His fingers grazed her hair, creating a ripple.

"Sadism," she answered from inside her retreat.

"Am I that hard to get along with?" He parted her hair in front so he could see her face.

Why were his eyes shining as if the sight of her delighted him? Eric Bellamy could have any female he wanted, and he interviewed plenty of beautiful women for their hip, glossy magazine.

"Hard to get along with?" she repeated. "Hard on my ego, that's for sure."

"You don't have an ego," he murmured. "Just immense talent, a lot of guts, and did I mention your fantastic breasts?"

She blushed as if on cue. "Not recently."

Tenderly, Eric brushed a kiss across her eyelids. His hands smoothed away the cascade of her hair and he leaned down until she felt his warm breath on her throat. With almost painful pleasure, his lips seized her nipples.

Anne succumbed without a struggle to the fire searing her. Never mind that she'd been struggling to establish a career in magazine journalism while Eric, a year younger than she, had simply breezed in and become a star. Never mind that his smooth manner and smashing good looks had made her distrust him from the start.

The man worked magic. He transformed her shyness into passion and her restraint into voluptuousness.

She grasped his hips and felt the tight pumping of his buttocks as he accepted her invitation. They joined in a burst of molten lava.

Anne lost all awareness of anything but Eric. His scent, his mouth, his teasing and thrusting.

He ravished her with a combination of skill and

instinct that made her forget the few men who had come before. There was no one like Eric. There never would be again.

When at last they lay quietly in each others' arms, he held her tight. "I've never met anyone like you. You're so...real."

"Real?" That adjective didn't rate very high on her list of favorite compliments.

"Genuine," he amended. "With you, I feel like I'm becoming the person I was meant to be."

"Instead of what?" she murmured into his shoulder.

"I don't know," he admitted. "I guess at twenty-five I should know who I am, but in some ways I'm still trying to define myself."

"My lover," she whispered. "That's who you are."

He chuckled deep in his throat. "Listen, it's nearly eleven. I've got to shower and turn in that story. Why don't you take the day off? I'll tell Laurie you've got a bad cold or something. After work, I'll pick up some Chinese food and we can resume where we left off."

Anne never called in sick, even when she really was. She was always one of the first staffers in the office, full of story proposals, afraid of missing an opportunity.

Maybe she tried too hard. Maybe she ought to be more laid-back, like Eric. "You're sure you don't mind?"

"Not a bit." He kissed her forehead. "I want to coddle you and do special things for you. Let's start with letting you sleep in."

A twinge of worry, or maybe it was guilt, nagged

at her. This story was special and would attract a lot of attention for *CoolNotes*. Shouldn't she be there when it was handed in?

The magazine's planned cover story had dropped out at the last minute when its subject, a hot young singer-actress, threw a temper tantrum over some minor detail and refused to pose for photographs. Laurie, an experienced editor in her early forties, might be high-handed but she knew her stuff, and she'd quickly come up with a replacement idea.

Some of Anne's earlier interviews, plus one by Eric, had been bumped from publication when the subjects' TV shows were canceled or their CDs fizzled. Laurie gave them three days to update the stories and pull together a piece about damaged Hollywood dreams, under the title "Has-beens and Hopefuls." For the cover, the art editor would assemble a photo collage.

With only the weekend left before the deadline, Eric had more or less moved into Anne's apartment. His own place might be bigger, but it came with a roommate, frequent phone calls from friends and relatives, and a nonstop party atmosphere.

She'd provided experience, a hard-won list of contacts and her honed writing skills. Eric brought flare and an edgy, high-energy style that made the story irresistible. To Anne's surprise, they'd made a dynamite team, even before last night's bedtime adventure.

"See you around six," Eric said. "Miss me?"

"What, already?" she teased.

"I miss *you*," he said. "I wish I didn't have to go." He hesitated on the threshold, then hurried outside with his laptop under one arm. The door clicked behind him.

Anne lay against the pillow and wondered if fairy tales could come true. She'd never imagined herself with a man like this; their backgrounds were so different, it was amazing they'd even met.

Her father had died when she was seven, leaving her mother struggling to support two children on a teacher's salary. Even though Anne had worked while attending college, she owed thousands of dollars in student loans, and she wanted to help her brother, Wayne, achieve his dream of attending medical school.

Eric, on the other hand, had been born into an immensely wealthy Chicago clan. His father, William "Budge" Bellamy, was a self-made, much-married millionaire known as The Pretzel King of North America.

There was an older brother and several step- and half brothers and sisters, whom Eric spoke of with affection. He obviously valued close relationships; he'd even anguished over breaking up with his girlfriend from college, a socialite named Caroline who sounded snobbish and completely wrong for him.

Anne's first impression had been that Eric was spoiled, but in the past few days he'd shown his sweet, playful side. She was beginning to hope he might care for her as much as she was beginning to care for him.

She didn't realize she was drifting off to sleep until the phone woke her. Groggily, she checked the time as she reached for it.

Three o'clock. Good heavens! "Hello?" she said thickly.

"Anne! How are you feeling?" Laurie didn't bother to identify herself. Her crisp, staccato voice was instantly recognizable, anyway.

"Tired," Anne said.

Having used up her meager supply of small talk, the editor continued, "I wanted to explain how we're going to handle this article."

"Handle it?" She wriggled into a sitting position. "What do you mean?"

"It's great, by the way!" Laurie continued. "With your legwork and Eric's talent, well, it'll make a splash!"

"Do we get bylines on the cover?" It would give Anne's career a boost.

"That's what I wanted to talk to you about." The editor coughed.

It wasn't like Laurie to beat around the bush. "You wanted to talk to me about our bylines?"

"I've decided to give Eric the byline on the main story and credit the sidebar to you."

Anne felt as if she'd been kicked in the stomach. The sidebar was a minor accompanying article. Not only would she not get recognized for co-writing the cover story, but sidebar bylines were so small, they were practically invisible.

"Wait a minute!" she said. "We worked on that piece together."

"Yes, I'm aware of that. Hang on—somebody has a question." The editor put her on hold and came back on the line a moment later. "I don't like double bylines on the cover, they're messy and boring."

"Boring?"

"Let's face it," Laurie added, "Eric's creating a stir around town. People notice him. He's becoming a celebrity in his own right, and that's good for the magazine.''

"So this is purely a matter of impressing the right people?" Anne demanded. "It has nothing to do with who wrote the article?"

"Oh, come on, Anne," Laurie snapped. "You're a good writer, but Eric's work sparkles. I can see his touch in this story and I think he deserves to have his name in lights."

It was true that Eric could jazz up even the most mundane interview. It was also true that without Anne's thorough research and attention to detail, the result would have been superficial and, in several instances, inaccurate.

But she didn't want to run him down. That wasn't the point.

"This is an unprofessional way to treat your writers," she said. "It's also unfair."

"I've made my decision," Laurie snapped.

"I've made mine, too," said Anne. "I quit." She hung up without waiting for an answer.

Rage burning in her chest, she hugged her knees and tried to stop the tears. She felt powerless and hurt. After three years at *CoolNotes,* she deserved better than this. Moreover, magazine jobs were hard to find, and she couldn't afford to be out of work, so she might have to take a position in public relations or technical writing.

A half hour of furious weeping later, she had exhausted a box of tissues and some of her distress. At times like this, her impulse was to call her mother, but Mom would still be teaching.

When the phone rang, she nearly didn't answer.

The reporter in her couldn't ignore it, though, so she picked it up.

Eric's voice sent quivers through her. "I can't believe what Laurie's doing! She told me you quit!"

"That's right." Her jaw was so stiff, it ached when she spoke.

"I think this is rotten," he said.

"Did you tell her so?"

"Of course!" He sounded confused and apologetic. "I asked her to take my name off, too, but she refused."

Anne tried to be generous. "The truth is, she doesn't value my work. I guess this is just a hard way to find out."

"That's not true!" Eric said. "She wants you to reconsider."

"She told you that?"

"Absolutely. This last-minute rush has put her behind on the next issue, and she says she relies on you to fill in the gaps."

Why wasn't Laurie explaining this herself instead of leaving the task to Eric? Anne wondered. "I'll come back if she changes her mind about the byline."

He released a long breath. "She won't do that. I tried to persuade her, but I got nowhere."

"You could quit, too." It was asking a lot, maybe too much. Still, the mere threat might be effective.

"I wish I could," Eric said. "But I swore when I came out to California that I was going to prove to my father that I could succeed on my own. I'm hoping in a few years to start my own magazine and I'll need to borrow money from him. I need credentials and experience, and where else am I going to get them?''

He needed credentials? What about her?

An ugly suspicion nagged at Anne. Was it possible this business of getting a sole byline was Eric's idea?

If he really wanted to share credit on the cover, surely he could have arranged it. While Laurie was tough with her other staff members, Eric had a knack for twisting the editor around his little finger.

Come to think of it, he was the one who'd suggested that Anne stay home while he turned in the article. Had he planned this all along? Had he even manipulated her...

...into bed?

"Anne?" he said worriedly. "Talk to me."

"I can't," she said.

"Why not?"

She swallowed hard and forced the words out. "You planned this, didn't you?"

"What?"

She could hardly find a way to express the magnitude of his betrayal. "You wanted to make a splash, and you didn't care who you used along the way. Isn't that right?"

"What are you talking about?" Eric sounded young and vulnerable.

About as vulnerable as a boa constrictor, she reminded herself. "Don't call me again."

"You think I set you up?" he said. "Anne, I wouldn't do that!"

"The facts speak for themselves." She hated arguing like this. She wanted to lie in his arms and cry, and let him reassure her. Yet, how could she believe him?

"I'm coming over," he said. "I'll bring dinner."

"I won't be here." She might as well move in with her mother, anyway. The rent was due in a few days, and without a job, she couldn't afford it.

"Anne! Give me a chance!"

"Goodbye, Eric." Her jaw aching with regret, she hung up.

He taught her a costly lesson about trust, but she was a quick learner, Anne told herself. He wouldn't fool her twice.

She weighed the merits of marching down to *CoolNotes* and confronting Laurie in person. Anne felt fairly certain she could get her job back.

And get kicked around the next time it suited the editor? Eric wasn't the only one to blame in this mess. Laurie had revealed more than she intended when she said she relied on Anne to fill in the gaps. Old Faithful, like a well-worn shoe. But well-worn shoes never got shown off like new favorites.

Anne would rather start over somewhere else. Make a name for herself or, at least, work with people who respected her and treated her decently.

She headed for the closet to start packing.

Chapter One

Across the lawn dotted with pastel-clad party goers, Anne saw Eric's head come up and caught the astonished glimmer in his eye. He'd spotted her.

A muscle worked in his chiseled jaw, and the June breeze ruffled his thick brown hair. In the five years since she'd seen him, he'd only gotten better looking.

Did he have to be so obvious? Surely everyone at the party noticed the way he was staring at her and how his tall, well-built body tightened inside his silk suit.

Anne supposed that sexual response was a spontaneous part of Eric's nature. It had nothing to do with love, obviously.

The worst part was her own instinctive reaction. As if they'd made love only last week, she could feel his hot breath on her throat and his mouth closing over her nipples.

She had to fight the urge to dig inside her handbag and pull out the blood pressure device she carried to help her employer. Today, she was the one with the high blood pressure, she felt certain.

California was two thousand miles away from this idyllic resort hotel in Lake Geneva, Wisconsin. In psychic distance, it might as well be on another planet.

Talk about feeling out of place! Anne's bargain-basement beige suit might serve for everyday, but among these thousand-dollar garden-party dresses, she felt like Cinderella watching her stepsisters preen.

Eric, however, was in his element. After returning to Chicago, he'd founded a successful, trendy magazine called *The Loop.* All you had to do was look at him—the perfectly fitted summer suit, the broad shoulders, the arrogant tilt of his head—to know he reigned over this scene.

She'd long ago gotten over him, of course. Any tattered remains of emotion would be buried forever this weekend, sans eulogy but amid plenty of flowers. Tons and tons of them, as befitted the society wedding of the year.

Eric's wedding. To his college girlfriend, hotel heiress, Caroline Lambert Knox.

Anne didn't want to be here. She certainly didn't want to be serving here as assistant to the bride's mother. However, real people had to work for a living, and she was no exception.

For three years after leaving *CoolNotes,* Anne had eked out a living freelancing articles, press releases and advertising copy, whatever would pay the rent. She'd been willing to take chances to get her magazine-writing career on track, and two years ago those efforts had landed her in Chicago, penniless and jobless, with a broken-down car.

Genevieve Lambert Knox paid her social secretaries well—she had to; otherwise nobody would handle the thousands of details of her charity work for her—and in desperation, Anne had signed on. The first year had gone quickly. Although Genevieve intimidated most people, there was plenty to like beneath the crusty surface, and Anne enjoyed not having to scramble for income.

Then, a year ago, came the stunning announcement that Caroline was going to marry her on-again-off-again boyfriend, Eric. If Anne hadn't needed the money so badly, and if she hadn't seen Genevieve on the verge of collapse over the prospect of planning the wedding, she might have left.

Instead, she slaved behind the scenes all year to help her employer arrange this event. Now the agony was almost over.

Last month, Anne's brother had graduated from medical school, and this month the last of her college loans would be paid off. She planned to stay a few months longer and save money while she applied for reporting jobs.

In the meantime, why should she mind watching Eric Bellamy marry his rather stuck-up bride? The prince had found the princess he deserved.

As for Cinderella, she was thinking of subscribing to a dating service.

WHAT ON EARTH was Anne Crumm doing here?

She'd exchanged her California casual tops and jeans for a tailored suit, and her swingy light-brown hair had been cut to chin-length. She looked a lot more collected than she had five years ago. Still as intense, though, with that lift of the chin, and that fire in her green eyes, Eric thought.

No one had ever inflamed him the way Anne did. For an instant, he ached to lower her onto a couch as he'd done that night long ago, to spread her hair across the cushions and crush her mouth beneath his.

Eric felt his body grow hard. Damn it, he shouldn't be reacting this way. Not now. Not when he'd finally accepted that, yes, he did intend to marry Caroline and that, no, he didn't mind that she'd more or less manipulated him into it. After all, he knew how much she needed him.

This should have been the happiest time of Eric's life. He was surrounded by beloved members of his scattered family, who come together for the union of Chicago's trendiest magazine publisher—him—and the glamorous heiress to a hotel chain.

Then why did he feel high-spirited one minute and out of sorts the next, and so restless he could hardly stand still? Ever since he'd arrived this morning, he'd been on edge, as if waiting for something to happen.

Well, it had happened. In spades. Anne Crumm was here.

Fortunately, his cool blond fiancée didn't notice anything amiss. A dozen feet away, she posed with one hand on the back of a white wrought-iron settee, forming a picture of elegance in her floating pink dress. The breeze barely stirred a hair from her up-swept coiffure.

She was listening with strained patience to her cousin and bridesmaid, Petronella "Petsy" Lambert Thorpe, coo gibberish at a four-year-old boy. With his jam-smeared face, the urchin bore little resemblance to the tuxedoed ring bearer he was to become on Saturday.

"Oosa little Lambie-pie coochy coochy lov'um Mumsy?" Petsy babbled at her son, Lambert. He stuck out his tongue and lobbed a pastry at her.

Eric wondered where the kid had found something edible. All he'd located so far were watercress sandwiches, dry biscuits that a waiter called scones, and unidentifiable pink hors d'oeuvres.

It wasn't hunger that was bothering him most, however. It was a restless curiosity.

He needed to find out what Anne was doing here. Across the party scene, he caught her eye and jerked his head toward the hotel, indicating that she should meet him inside.

In private, one last time.

"THAT'S THE GROOM, Eric Bellamy." Genevieve's stentorian voice turned the heads of a couple of swans lazing on the pond that meandered around two sides of the grounds. "I don't believe you've met my future son-in-law, have you? You never seem to be around when he comes to call."

"He's very handsome." Anne watched her employer snare another cup of tea from a waiter. Since Genevieve's family owned the hotel, she'd had no trouble arranging for her tea to be spiked. "Do you really think alcohol goes well with your blood-pressure medication?"

"I'm having a hot flash," said the woman.

"Scotch cools you?"

"It makes me feel younger," Genevieve said. "Oh, how I envy Caroline! To be so beautiful, and in love. I don't think she appreciates that man, to tell you the truth. Do you?"

"I wouldn't know." Anne had spent the past year, since the engagement was announced, hiding behind potted palms and darting into closets on the few occasions when Eric visited the Knox mansion during the daytime.

"I don't understand why she doesn't act more affectionate. He's such a perfect male specimen!" said Genevieve. "If she's not careful, some other woman's going to steal him from right under her nose."

Anne refrained from pointing out that Genevieve rarely showed any warmth toward her own husband. Johnny Hainsworth Knox had been a bellboy before he married the boss's daughter and rose to become CEO of the Lambert Hotel empire.

Right now, the silver-haired father of the bride was, she noticed, carrying on a desultory conversation with one of the guests. His wistful glances toward his wife went unnoticed.

"I don't know whether my daughter appreciates all our hard work, but we've made sure she's going to have the perfect wedding," Genevieve continued. "Don't you think everyone's having a good time?"

"The party's going splendidly." As if Swan's Folly, the flagship facility of the hotel chain, wouldn't turn itself inside out for the wedding of its CEO's daughter!

Matters were complicated by Caroline's insistence on choosing whatever suited her fancy, be it kitschy bridesmaid dresses or froufrou refreshments, without regard for anyone else's opinion. Genevieve had bowed to most of her demands, and out of her daughter's hearing, relieved her frustrations by complaining to her assistant.

Personally, Anne didn't care whether the ninety-odd guests were enjoying the overly sweet pink punch and matching pink appetizers; or whether the much feared paparazzi were going to crash the gates to harass the happy couple. She simply wanted to keep her stressed-out employer upright and functioning.

It was her duty to follow Genevieve's orders, keep track of numerous checklists, and discreetly smooth her employer's path. What made the job so difficult was that it relied as much on intuition and tact as on Anne's secretarial skills.

Across the sloping lawn, Eric's gaze held hers. Sharply, he nodded toward the hotel's main building, an English-style country house.

He wanted to talk to her. Well, why not? This Thursday afternoon garden party was supposed to be an icebreaker for the three days of wedding festivities, so she and Eric might as well break the ice.

The problem was figuring out how to detach herself from Genevieve for a few minutes. Eric was already disappearing into the building.

"Your hat!" Anne said to Genevieve, suddenly inspired.

Her boss grabbed her gauzy brim as if to steady it. "What's wrong with it?"

"Loose thread."

"Oh, is that all?" Her employer exhaled in relief. "I'm sure you've got a scissors in that purse of yours."

As a matter of fact, she did, right on the Swiss Army knife. "I left it in the suite. I'll run and get it."

"You're leaving me?" The older woman clutched her arm. Despite her confident carriage and haughty manner, Genevieve needed someone to lean on. Too bad she hadn't chosen to make that someone her husband, Anne thought.

"Five minutes," she said. "Oh, there's your mother! Doesn't she look lovely?"

"She looks like a crackpot, which is what she is," grumbled Genevieve.

Eighty-two-year-old Isabella Lambert, better known as Nana, believed herself to be the reincarnation of Isadora Duncan, even though she'd been born ten years before the famous dancer's death. A vision in lavender from her print scarf to her high ankle-strapped shoes, the eccentric octogenarian teetered on the arm of a young man.

"She's charming," said Anne.

"I'd better go make sure she doesn't break her neck." Visibly shrinking from queen of Chicago society to dutiful daughter, Genevieve set aside her teacup and trudged toward the dowager.

With her boss occupied, Anne headed for the hotel's brick terrace at a near run.

AFTER THE SUMMER sunshine, it took her eyes a moment to adjust to the wood-paneled lobby. In the dimness, Anne was struck by the rich scents wafting from the large floral displays. No doubt the greenhouses of the entire Midwest would be stripped bare by the time Saturday's ceremony concluded.

Then she caught sight of Eric, fidgeting at the foot of the curving staircase. His restless movements, coupled with his well-built frame, gave him the look of a Thoroughbred in need of exercise.

Anne had spent the past year trying not to speculate about what kind of exercise he was getting with Caroline. From the looks of him, it wasn't nearly enough. Maybe one woman never would be, for a man like him.

His eyes raked over her, and he grew still. The keenness of his focus took her breath away.

His magnetism radiated across the lobby. Even though she knew how untrustworthy this man could be, he retained the power to capture her in his net and draw her, unwillingly, toward him.

"Anne! I couldn't believe it was you." His strong hands caught her slender ones. "What are you doing here?"

"Working." She tried not to gaze too deeply into those melting eyes. Not to let herself feel his intense male heat.

"As a reporter?" he asked. "I thought the only one here was from my magazine."

She knew she should tell him the truth immediately, but she enjoyed giving him the impression he'd been one-upped. "Do you think your staff writers are the only ones who know how to get a story?"

"Not at all. In fact, I expected you to be famous by now." He oozed sincerity. And heart-wrenching charm; Anne could feel herself falling under his spell. *No. Not this time.* "Maybe have a Pulitzer to your credit."

His speculation was so far from the truth that she could have laughed. Or cried. Didn't he realize how difficult this field was for someone without wealth, connections or flashy good looks?

Of course not. Eric saw what he wanted to see and believed what he wanted to believe. Otherwise he would have noticed the complete absence of her by-line from any known publications during the past two years.

"Oh, give me a few more weeks," she joked. "I understand the Pulitzer committee can't decide which of my investigative series they should honor."

A group of people passed by, some of them greeting Eric by name. After responding in distracted fashion, he said, "We need to be alone."

"Not a good idea."

"But necessary." He pulled Anne down the hallway into a room redolent of pipe smoke. From the pool table in the middle, she gathered that this was the billiards room she'd seen on the hotel's layout chart.

"I can't stay," she said. "I have other obligations." At any moment, Nana might decide to perform the dance of the seven veils. "Besides, I told you, I don't think it's wise for us to meet this way."

"I wish you had let me talk to you five years ago. I couldn't find you," Eric said. "What did you do, take off that night and have your phone disconnected the next morning?"

"I moved in with my mother." As Anne spoke, all the turbulent emotions rushed back. She found it hard to believe that five years had passed and that Eric was engaged to someone else. "It seemed like a practical step while I job hunted. Do you mean you actually looked for me?"

"Of course I did!"

"Well, I'm sure you had a rough hour or two until you gave up."

"Believe me, I've given a lot of thought to what happened." He stood much too close; she could smell his expensive aftershave and the masculinity beneath it. "I hadn't considered until then how the situation might strike you. The truth is, I wasn't used to seeing things from another person's perspective."

"Are you now?" she asked. "Seriously?"

Eric ducked his head, acknowledging a direct hit. "No, not entirely. But at the time, it was a completely new experience. Maybe that's why it took me so long to see that you were right."

"About what?"

"Don't get me wrong, I didn't set you up. I'm not that rotten." His breath tickled her neck, reminding her of shared intimacies. "But you were right when you suggested that I should quit my job. Laurie was unfair, and I let her get away with it."

His humility touched her. On the other hand, what was to be gained by a reconciliation at this point? "That's water under the bridge. You went your way and I went mine, and here we are, still afloat."

His thumb brushed her cheek. "Yes, here we are, aren't we?"

Anne took a step backward and discovered she'd become wedged between Eric and the pool table. "In the billiards room."

"*Alone* in the billiards room," he murmured, his mouth descending toward hers.

"The billiards room that belongs to your fiancée's family." The words came out in a rush. "As does the rest of Swan's Folly."

He blinked as if clearing a haze. "You always had a way of bringing me down to earth. Thank you."

"You certainly brought *me* down to earth," she said. "I'm happy to return the favor. Is there anything else you wanted to say? Otherwise, I have to go. I'm working, remember?"

Sudden suspicion narrowed his eyes. "Wait a minute. Are you taking notes about this encounter?"

Of all the ridiculous accusations! "Do you see a pad in my hand?" she snapped.

"You could be hiding a tape recorder in that purse. It's big enough."

He sounded as if he were half joking, but this slam at Anne's professional integrity offended her. "Maybe that's your idea of journalism, Eric Bellamy, but it isn't mine! What do you think I work for, some scandal sheet?"

With the heel of his hand, he shoved a lock of hair off his forehead. "I'm sorry. You're right. You'd never lower yourself to such cheap tricks." His contrite air lasted only an instant before it was replaced by a gleam of curiosity. "Exactly what *do* you carry in that suitcase?"

She angled it behind her. "My minicam."

"You wouldn't have anything to eat, by chance?"

Anne couldn't suppress a grin. "You mean, you don't like watercress finger delicacies and salmon surprise?"

"Is that what those hors d'oeuvres are? Come on, you must have a stash of candy bars in there. As one reporter to another, you can't leave me to starve!" Eric feinted toward the bag, and Anne felt the touch of hard thigh and hip as he pressed her against the padded edge of the pool table.

She nearly lost her balance, until his grip steadied her arm. At the contact, her pulse speeded up and her knees threatened to buckle.

The billiards room, she noticed, came with a deep, inviting leather sofa. She would feel better if she could sit down. Maybe lie down. Preferably with Eric beside her...

"Are you thinking what I'm thinking?" he asked.

She swallowed. This entire scenario was wrong, emotionally, morally and in every other way. "Aren't you forgetting something?"

"I'm trying not to." Ruefully, he removed his hand from her elbow. "Until I saw you a few minutes ago, I was perfectly happy."

"Aren't you, now?" she couldn't resist asking.

"Well, sure. Caroline's a special person. There's a bond between us." He spoke slowly, choosing his words. "I'd almost forgotten that you and I—how I felt—Anne, I shouldn't be talking this way. I don't know what's come over me."

"I do," she said. "Grooms are notorious for developing last-minute jitters."

"Is that what this is?" He studied her for a moment before adding, "You must be right."

A soprano voice with a finishing-school accent wafted from the hall. "Eric? Eric, are you in there?"

"You've been missed." Anne scrambled as far away from him as the furniture would allow, and glanced around in vain for another exit.

"I'm sorry." From his expression, he might have been a small boy caught sneaking cookies before dinner. "Are you going to report this? It would be no more than I deserve."

"Report?" Guiltily, Anne remembered that she hadn't corrected his false impression of her employment. "No, I'm not..."

"Here you are!" In marched Caroline. If Eric was a Thoroughbred, Genevieve's daughter was a greyhound, sleekly groomed and whippet-thin. "So this is where you wandered off to! I turned to speak to you and you weren't there. Do you know how embarrassing that was?''

"I was just renewing acquaintances with—" his jaw worked, as he sought a simple explanation and apparently didn't find one "—with Anne," he concluded. "Have you met?"

"Of course we've met," snapped Caroline. "She's my mother's secretary. Now let's get back to the party before people start to gossip!"

At Eric's stunned expression, Anne felt her cheeks get hot. Not that there was any shame in working as a personal assistant, but she had let him believe she was still a journalist.

Now he understood that, in professional terms, she was no longer his equal. She was someone that his bride's mother ordered around, someone who fetched and carried for Genevieve, someone beneath Caroline's notice.

The bride-to-be piloted her fiancé out the door with a firm grip. To Anne's relief, he didn't look back.

This humiliation was her own fault for clinging to false pride. There was no reason to hide the fact that she earned an honest living as a secretary, paying off her debts and helping her younger brother through school.

She doubted Eric would find any reason to speak to her privately again, however, now that he knew the truth. As for her, she intended to stay as far away from him as possible for the rest of the weekend.

Chapter Two

As Eric marched along the corridor beside Caroline, he struggled to get a grip on his seething emotions. Why had Anne left journalism? What was she doing in the Midwest? And why did he care so much?

For five years, she'd made cameo appearances in his dreams. Finally he'd convinced himself that he was projecting his needs into a fantasy image. If he ever did run into her again, he'd told himself he would undoubtedly be disappointed.

So much for his ability to predict the future. A minute ago, he'd wanted Anne with a passion he'd never felt for another woman, including his future wife. It wasn't simply sex, either.

Eric missed Anne's quick wit. Her skepticism. The way she stood up to him, something few had dared to do since he founded *The Loop* and set local records for circulation growth.

He had to stop thinking this way. He couldn't hurt the woman who loved and trusted him, and who needed him in ways that a strong woman like Anne never would.

"Is something wrong?" asked Caroline as she

towed him to a trellis interlaced with climbing roses. "You act as if you hardly know I'm here."

Eric shook his head to clear it. "I'm sorry." It would, truth to tell, be difficult to ignore Caro's statuesque presence and classic beauty. "Are you having a good time, dear? I mean, aside from my inexcusable lapses?"

"I would be, if half the guests weren't missing! How could they abandon me this way?"

Over the years, Eric had learned to estimate crowd size with fair accuracy. A sweeping survey of this one put the tally at close to eighty. "I'd say almost everyone was here."

Caroline's thin lips twisted. "Two of my bridesmaids haven't arrived! Maybe they aren't coming."

She was right. Neither Eric's former stepsister, Bianca, nor Caro's college roommate, Lizzie, had made an appearance. Fondly, he reflected that each marched to her own drummer. Each was, in her own way, a remarkable lady.

"Of course they're coming. They wouldn't want to miss the most beautiful wedding of the year." He gestured at the sunny cheer of the onetime country estate.

The velvety grass, the banks of flowers and the meandering pond with its curvaceous flock of swans set an appealing scene. The Folly, a mock ruin that resembled an old castle, might be a bit pretentious but it added to the fairy-tale effect.

His bride had chosen it with unerring good taste. Even the way she now positioned the two of them here beneath the rose arbor presented the image of a storybook couple.

Images and aspirations. That was what filled the

pages of *The Loop,* and Caroline understood them. Sometimes better than Eric did. No wonder people said the two of them suited each other perfectly. So why did he keep wishing he could hear Anne make some humorous crack about phony castles and inedible hors d'oeuvres?

The official wedding photographer, a middle-aged man in a brown suit, paused to take pictures before continuing discreetly on his way. Eric hoped he was being thorough; his work would also accompany the write-up in *The Loop.*

"Sure, Cousin Petsy's here, and so is my sister," Caro said in his ear. "They have to be here, they're relatives. But what could be delaying Lizzie? And you should never have suggested I ask Bianca to join the wedding party. She's such a flake!"

She broke off to bestow a smile on Eric's father. Budge Bellamy, a bulldozer of a man clad in tennis whites, saluted her jauntily, gave his son a nod and continued on his path toward the tennis courts.

Although the party was getting into full swing, Budge had never been one to worry about other people's opinions or to stick around if he got bored. His fifth wife, Rhonda, and their five-year-old daughter must be here somewhere, since little Fawn was to be the wedding's flower girl, but, as usual, Budge was leaving them to fend for themselves.

A wave of guilt washed over Eric. Hadn't he been doing the same thing to Caro, following his own inclinations and giving little thought to her?

He didn't want to live the way his father did, casually discarding wives, arranging everything to suit himself. Particularly not when it came to Caroline who, despite her sharp manner, was quite fragile underneath.

If he'd learned anything from his disastrous affair with Anne, it was the importance of loyalty. Unfortunately, he'd never had a chance to demonstrate it to her. Caroline, however, would benefit from his hard lesson.

He'd given her a promise. Well, he'd given her a ring, anyway, which amounted to the same thing. And he intended to live up to it.

"Honey, I'm sorry I left the party that way," he said. "As for suggesting my stepsister—former stepsister—as a bridesmaid, I was trying to do Bianca and my brother a favor. I wanted to throw them into each other's paths, which is practically impossible with her living overseas."

"You're matchmaking?" said his bride. "Well, I think it's a waste of time, but suit yourself."

"I'll be careful." During the turbulent course of their ten-year relationship, Eric had learned not to let Caro's strong opinions bother him. When she was happy, she radiated a charisma that made others envy her, but he'd seen the frightened little girl who still dwelled inside.

In Eric's pocket, the cell phone rang. Since his whole family was present today, it had to be an emergency at the office. "I'd better get that."

"Not another interruption!" said Caroline.

"This will only take a minute." He flipped it open. "Yes?"

"It's Gabby." Gabby Greer, a chubby redhead with an upturned nose, was in charge of traffic at *The Loop,* an essential post that involved making sure everything got routed and completed properly. She'd also taken on extra duties while the assistant editor recovered from thyroid surgery. "Sorry to interrupt, but we have a major problem with the September article on the rent-a-date service."

"What kind of problem?"

"Does the word *libel* mean anything to you?"

Caro was making annoyed faces at him. "Pull the story," Eric said.

"We can't! It's too late. There's no time to come up with new illustrations, and besides, it's a theme issue, remember? 'Romance at the Turn of the Millennium.' We can't simply drop in some evergreen article from our files."

"Eric!" said his bride-to-be. "Would you please get off the phone?"

Across the lawn, he saw his stepsister Bianca arrive, at last. Her black dress stood out against the pastels of the other guests, and she was pushing a baby carriage.

That ought to get his brother Neill's attention. If not, he couldn't imagine what would.

Eric peered past her, trying to spot the one person he needed: Montcrief DeLong, twenty-four-year-old hotshot reporter for *The Loop* and author of the offending article. He was supposed to be here covering the wedding weekend. "I'll put Monty on it as soon as I find him."

"That party boy? What do you think he'd accomplish? He's the clown who screwed it up in the first place!" Now he remembered why he'd hired Gabby; her forthrightness reminded him of Anne. "We need a rewrite by someone who has a nodding acquaintance with nonfiction."

Eric had done his best to tie up loose ends at the

magazine before he left. He'd cleared the next two weeks, although he didn't yet know Caroline's plans for the honeymoon. They'd been so busy these past few weeks, they scarcely saw each other. ''I'll have to, uh—''

''Please get off the phone!'' demanded his fiancée.

He covered the mouthpiece with his hand. ''Give me another minute. It's urgent.''

''Off! Now!'' She was working herself into a fit.

Angling the receiver away, he said, ''Gabby, I'll get back to you. Don't worry, I'll—''

''Now!'' cried the overwrought bride, and grabbing the phone from his hand, clicked it off.

Eric understood Caro. Like him, she was a perfectionist, and the struggle to meet the high expectations of herself and others sometimes created a high level of stress.

But she never interfered in his work before, or treated him like one of her servants.

Fighting to keep his voice low, he caught her by the shoulders and forced her to look directly into his face. ''Don't—ever—do—that—again.''

She gasped. ''How dare you manhandle me?''

He released her as if she were on fire. ''I didn't mean to hurt you.''

''You've done nothing but ignore me all day! Don't you care about my feelings?'' In full view of her guests, she stormed across the lawn in the direction of the gazebo.

He had no choice but to follow. Nevertheless, Eric reflected as heads turned to observe this unfolding melodrama. He and Caroline had to clear up a few essential points.

A man needed to be treated with respect, just as a

woman did. Eric couldn't tolerate any less, not if they were going to spend their lives together.

If?

The word made him break stride. He didn't mean that, of course. He couldn't be entertaining doubts at this eleventh hour.

What was the explanation Anne had given? Grooms developed last-minute jitters. That must be what was happening to him.

He and Caro had been quarreling and reconciling ever since college. Her abrasive manner would be distancing, but then she would melt and confide her deepest fears. Only Eric knew her terrible fear of abandonment, because he was the only one she could talk to.

At the age of ten, she'd been sent to boarding school after her younger sister was badly injured in a car crash. Her parents must have believed that Caroline would enjoy her friends and horseback riding more than waiting in hospital rooms.

They hadn't realized that their focus on Winnie, and their reserved manner around their older daughter, had given her a profound sense of loss. Too proud to admit how much she ached to come home, she stayed away for four long years, until the start of high school.

Since then, the fear of rejection had colored her entire outlook on life. Knowing all this Eric could never betray Caroline, or hurt her. She depended on him too much.

He started after her, to make peace one more time.

"I CAN'T BELIEVE they're fighting!" Genevieve made a helpless gesture in midair. "Anne, make them stop!"

"Why me?" Sitting on a bench pretending to trim a string from the hat in her lap, Anne hoped no one had tattled about seeing her talking with Eric in the hotel. The last thing she needed was questions from her employer.

"Why you?" echoed that booming female voice. "Because you're so capable. So calm. Even when things fall apart, it never bothers you."

Nothing bothered her, Anne mused as she bent over Genevieve's hat—snipping away the nonexistent piece of thread—because the things that troubled Genevieve didn't matter. Her employer went into a tizzy over waiters who served champagne in wineglasses, social climbers who crashed charity balls and men who sported black ties when they should have worn tuxedos.

Emotionally, Genevieve lived in a house of cards that frequently came tumbling down. Fear of losing control turned her into a high-handed tyrant; to keep her job, Anne had learned to unruffle feathers and set things right with a combination of efficiency and humor.

Until today, that hadn't been difficult. Even now, she refused to let an old heartache get in the way of duty.

"Things aren't falling apart." Rising to her feet, she set the hat atop her employer's silvery-blond pageboy. "Your daughter and her fiancé are always squabbling. You said so yourself."

"I suppose you're right." Genevieve adjusted the brim. "How do I look? Too young? Too old?"

"For what?" asked Anne.

Her employer shrugged. "Nothing in particular."
She peeked toward the edge of the pond, where her
dapper husband stood conversing with an animated
young woman.

As usual, Hainsworth managed to focus on his
companion and keep an eye on his surroundings at
the same time. He was, no doubt, making sure the
Swan's Folly staff handled its job with panache.

The hotel CEO had always impressed Anne with
his calm air of command. Usually, however, Genevieve hardly seemed aware he was around. What had
happened to the sizzling rich girl-poor boy romance
that led them to marry?

And why the change now? Could their daughter's
wedding be awakening old desires?

Apparently so, because her employer's next words
were, "Who is that woman flirting with Hainsworth?
I don't recognize her."

"That's Mrs. Wright. Her husband is a friend of
Budge Bellamy's," Anne replied, having memorized
the guest list.

"Oh, she's married." Genevieve sounded relieved. Did she believe her husband would cheat? He
was neither a fool nor a cad, although he might well
be lonely.

A moving figure drew Anne's attention to one side
of the garden. She glanced over in time to see Caroline stalk around a corner of the building and vanish. Eric, wearing a resigned expression, strode after
her.

The two of them hardly acted like lovebirds, yet
Eric must adore this woman. Why else would he be
marrying her?

Whether it was due to the excitement he'd aroused

or the pain he left behind, no other man had sparked Anne's interest since their night together. She hoped that seeing him this weekend, uncomfortable as it was, would finally free her to find someone else.

In the meantime, she had to keep a smile on her face, and be pleasant to the guests. This included Eric's mother, Vivian, who was sailing toward them.

"Good heavens, that hair!" muttered Genevieve, her tongue loosened by the Scotch. "How did a woman like that ever produce such a classy son?"

Everything about the mother of the groom, who had been married twice to Budge the Pretzel King, was larger than life. That included her expressive features and her newly dyed red hair.

The former housewife, after being dumped the second time for a much younger secretary, had reinvented herself as a sculptress specializing in life-size figures of men. Young, athletic, nude men.

"I want you to know," said Viv, coming abreast of them, "that I don't believe a word of it."

"A word of what, dear?" asked Genevieve. The two women had once moved in the same social circles, Anne recalled, although in view of their different temperaments, she couldn't imagine that they'd ever been friends.

"The rumors."

Genevieve's fists tightened as if she were preparing to do battle. "What sort of rumors?"

Oh, please don't let them be about me! she prayed.

"Who could forget the gossip last year at the engagement party?" Viv went on blithely. "You know, when my son turned up *ages* late, with his stepsister—former stepsister—hanging on his arm, and he said he'd gone to get a haircut and lost track of the time. Doesn't Bianca look lovely, by the way?"

She nodded toward a stunning blond woman who stood next to a baby carriage, talking to Nana. So that was Bianca. When they worked at *CoolNotes,* Eric had mentioned her to Anne a few times, sounding like a concerned older brother.

Genevieve drew herself up to her full height, which gave her the advantage over the other woman. "I understand she's been living in Rome or Paris or somewhere. I can't imagine what people could be spreading rumors about."

"Why, about the baby," murmured the mother of the groom. "Bianca's baby. It's exactly three months old. Let's see, nine months plus three makes a year, doesn't it?"

Judging by the color rising in her neck, Genevieve's blood pressure must be approaching the danger level. "It certainly isn't Eric's! If it were, he'd have told Caroline. And you, of course."

"Maybe he didn't know, with Bianca living so far away. She's always played her cards close to her chest," Viv said. "But then, with a chest like that, she probably has lots of boyfriends. As I said, I don't believe the rumors." Eric's mother excused herself and made a beeline for a new arrival, a well-built young man handsome enough to serve as a model.

"It can't be true!" Genevieve said tightly.

"Of course not," Anne agreed. "The girl is his stepsister."

"I don't believe they ever actually lived in the same household," fretted her boss. "Why do you suppose Eric insisted that Caroline ask Bianca to be a bridesmaid? Did he want an excuse to see her again?"

"If he had, he could have arranged it on his own," she said. "Besides, he certainly wouldn't have slept with her right before his engagement party! What kind of jerk would do that?"

"Even the best men can be susceptible." Genevieve's eyes narrowed. "Bianca has that cheap, sensual glow that makes fellows act like animals. I think she wants to break them up. She's been giving Eric the eye since she got here."

"If you ask me, the one she's been sneaking glances at is Eric's brother." Anne was glad she'd studied the photographs from the engagement party so she could recognize the players. She herself had feigned a sore throat and stayed home that evening.

Arguing with her boss was like trying to swim up a waterfall. "In the last few days before the wedding, a groom is practically defenseless against any scheming female," Genevieve grumbled.

"Eric? Defenseless?" Anne might accuse him of many things, but she would never cast him as a pushover. "Genevieve, you're doing what my mother calls Awfulizing. You're imagining every awful thing that could happen and dwelling on it."

Her employer steamrollered on. "Caroline *must* get married on Saturday. She's twenty-eight—nearly thirty! And Eric's the only man good enough for her."

"Of course they'll get married." Anne swallowed the lump in her throat.

"I've got it!" The tall woman spread her hands as if she'd received a divine inspiration. "You, Anne! You'll make sure everything stays on track!"

"If you like, I can help keep Bianca occupied."
She didn't relish acting as a nursemaid, literally or
figuratively. If her job required it, though, she would.

"I didn't just mean Bianca. Eric's a magnet for
women," Genevieve continued. "What if someone
else sneaks in while we're not looking? I told Caroline she should stay at Ivy Cottage with him, but
she said it wouldn't look right. So there she is in the
bridal suite, and he's across the grounds, all alone."

"Surely you don't believe he'd cheat on his
bride!"

Genevieve gave no sign of hearing her. Panic
must've clouded the woman's brain, aided no doubt
by the Scotch. "Someone has to make sure nothing
interferes with my daughter's happiness! Anne, you
have to spy on him!"

"What!"

A couple of new arrivals headed their way, clearly
expecting to be welcomed. "Make sure he stays on
the straight and narrow. I'm counting on you,
Anne!"

"I hardly know the man! I mean, I don't know
him at all."

"So? You know what he looks like, don't you?"
Barely pausing to catch her breath, Genevieve assumed her most sociable smile. "Madge! Rudolf! So
glad you could come!"

Anne stood rooted to the spot. She didn't see how
she could be expected to shadow Eric for the next
two days. Not only would it soon become obvious
that something odd was going on, but she couldn't
risk being that close to him for that long.

Maybe the whole foolish idea would slip Genevieve's mind before it became entrenched. She hoped

so, because once her employer fixated on a course of action, changing it would require either an act of Congress or a burning bush.

But, as the guests gushed over the party arrangements, Genevieve leaned to speak directly into Anne's ear. "Go find him and stick to him like glue! Anytime he isn't with my daughter, I expect you to be right behind him!" All uncertainty had vanished from her imperious manner. "Is that clear?"

"Perfectly," she said.

On the far side of the pond, Eric appeared, apparently en route to his cottage. There was no sign of Caroline. "After him!" growled her boss.

With an inward shudder, Anne went in pursuit.

Chapter Three

Caroline hadn't been in any mood to accept an apology. She was determined to punish him, and Eric found, for the first time since their engagement, that he couldn't find the words to reassure her.

Becoming aware that his patience was fraying, he'd walked away from the gazebo before he said anything that might hurt her further. Now, to avoid the guests at the garden party, he headed for his cottage, hugging the far side of the pond until a grove of willows blocked the lawn from view.

A few hours remained before the wedding rehearsal. He hoped that would be enough time for his future wife to calm down.

Embarking on a marriage wasn't the same as carrying on a dating relationship. Surely Caro would realize that he couldn't play the devoted slave twenty-four hours a day.

Besides, he was anxious to reach his room so he could call Gabby at the magazine. If Caroline had allowed him to finish his conversation the first time, he might not be in such a touchy frame of mind now.

After he squared matters at the office, he'd go jogging. He needed to burn off this edginess.

Eric had taken a dozen or so strides when, from the corner of his eye, he saw something move. He swung about and scanned the area. No one there.

The more he thought about it, though, the more certain he was that he'd seen someone. He always had excellent peripheral vision.

Had some member of the paparazzi sneaked through the gates? Eric's senses came to full alert.

Since his engagement to Caroline was announced last year, there'd been intense media scrutiny. For the first few weeks, swarms had greeted them wherever they went. One camera crew was arrested on the grounds of the Knox mansion. Outside Eric's penthouse, firemen had been called to rescue a photographer who ascended in window-washing equipment and then froze in fear.

The hysteria had died down for a while but resumed as the date approached. Although the hotel's discreet security staff was on full alert, some determined individual might have made it through.

The direct approach often worked best in flushing them out. Besides, being a member of the press himself, Eric retained a certain sympathy. "Hello?" he called.

Again, no answer. By now, a cameraman would have revealed himself by the soft whirr of a motorized lens. Could it be one of the groomsmen, instead?

If this was Neill's idea of a joke, Eric might repay the favor by short-sheeting his brother's bed. Or it could be his stepbrother, Joe. The old bucket-of-water-over-the-door trick would be the perfect revenge on him, since Joe was a firefighter.

A bit of shenanigans might relieve the tension, he

had to admit. Until now, he hadn't even realized he was tense.

He hoped he would be able to spend some time this weekend with Neill and Joe, to joke around and maybe find out whether either of those two confirmed bachelors had fallen in love yet. Or in Neill's case, when it came to Bianca, whether he was already in love.

Next to the walkway, a bush shivered. Eric snapped back to the present.

He was debating whether to sneak toward it when he remembered the swans that infested the hotel grounds. Graceful as they might be in water, the creatures showed their noisy, aggressive side on land. If he pounced on one, the racket would draw everyone's attention and make him a laughingstock for the rest of the weekend.

Cautiously, he resumed his stroll. For a short distance, he thought he was rid of whoever or whatever he'd heard, and then, quite distinctly, a twig broke.

When he peered back, he couldn't see through the dense foliage. Still, his pursuer didn't seem clumsy enough to be a swan.

Abandoning the path, he made his way through the trees. Behind him came a rustle. Careful to keep his movements casual, he tilted his head to watch the rear area.

There! Something white slipped behind a willow. It reminded Eric that he'd seen a white cat prowling the grounds that morning.

"Here, kitty, kitty," he tried.

Silence. Then: "Meow."

It was almost, but not quite, convincing. He was being followed by a person, all right.

Could it be Caroline, trying to jolly away the bad feelings by sneaking up on him? That would be a welcome step in the right direction.

At the possibility that she possessed a playful side, relief ran through Eric. He'd been wondering how they were going to endure fifty years without laughing together.

"Is that 'meow' as in, 'I'm hungry,' or 'meow' as in 'I want my tummy scratched'?" he asked.

"It's 'meow' as in I'm a cat and you don't know I'm here," came the squeaky reply.

"You don't want me to see you?"

"You can't. I'm an invisible cat," said the squeaky voice. "Now go away."

That didn't sound like Caroline. And now that he thought about it, she wasn't likely to risk snagging her expensive dress, or smudging her perfectly made-up face in the woods, either.

Whoever was pretending to be a cat, she sounded like more fun than his fiancée, he conceded reluctantly. "If I leave, will you follow me?"

A moment's contemplation, then: "Yes."

"Why?"

"That's what invisible cats do."

Then it hit him. Of course! It had to be Fawn, his little half sister, creeping around in the bushes pretending to be a kitty. The five-year-old flower girl must be bored silly by the grown-up party.

His twinge of disappointment that Caro wasn't showing a new side of herself gave way to amusement. Eric loved kids, and he felt an indulgent fondness toward his siblings.

Fawn adored being tickled. She was also quick and wiggly, so he'd have to be clever to catch her.

"I'd like to pet your soft fur. Can't I do that?" Muffling his footsteps on the grass, he slipped toward the shrubbery. Best to angle to one side, then close in on his little target.

"You can't pet me. Invisible cats don't have fur," squeaked the nest of leaves.

The kid was surprisingly articulate, Eric thought. He hadn't realized Fawn was so precocious. But the only other possibility who came to mind was Petsy's son, and Lambie could never keep still this long.

As he sneaked forward, he didn't dare speak again for fear of revealing his location. Fawn wouldn't hesitate to squirm along the ground to a safer hiding place, even if it meant ruining her party dress. His dad might laugh off the incident, but he doubted that Rhonda would.

Time to close in for the kill. He sprang forward and leaped atop the bush, shouting, "Gotcha!"

He had his hands on her—she twisted away—he pinned her with his body—she shrieked—he clamped down on...a full-grown woman.

Soft hair swung against his wrists. He inhaled the achingly familiar fragrance of flowers and femininity. Registered the flush of her cheeks and the reluctant laughter in her green eyes.

Then he lost his balance and they rolled, flailing and kicking, until they thumped against a tree trunk near the pond's edge. The creature in his arms heaved a sigh.

"So much for my Mata Hari gig," Anne said.

She lay beneath him, her breasts crushed against his chest, her legs tangling with his. Time dissolved and they were back in California, on the couch in her apartment, and Eric was young, free and wildly turned on.

"Oh, lord," he groaned.

"This position is a smidge too familiar," Anne mused, echoing his train of thought. She peered toward the party guests, some distance away on the other side of the pond. "Thank goodness those two kids just fell in the water. I don't think anybody noticed the fuss we made."

"What two kids?" Gazing partyward, he saw a couple of people dredging Fawn and Lambie from the drink. "Oh, them. They're always in trouble."

"Do you think you could get off me?"

"Will I get an explanation if I do?" It seemed wise to bargain before he committed himself.

"An explanation of what?"

"Of what you're doing here."

She frowned. "Define your terms. Do you mean why am I here wallowing in the dirt with you, or why am I here at Lake Geneva and why did I leave California?"

"Both," he said. "I mean, all of the above."

"You drive a hard bargain."

"It's my body that's driving a hard bargain," he said truthfully. "I'm still trying to figure out a way to remove myself without performing an act of irredeemable intimacy."

"Irredeemable intimacy?" she teased. "Could you spell that?"

"Not without a dictionary."

They both got the giggles. Or, in his case, the chuckles. Eric's knees went weak and for a moment, it seemed he truly never would succeed in removing himself from temptation.

He missed having conversations like this, where the wisecracks bounced back and forth like tennis balls. Anne always returned his serves with such smashing unpredictability that he ended up panting and sweating and—*No sense in finishing that thought,* he told himself.

Slowly he lifted himself away and sat up. Eric could see grass stains on the knees of his cream-colored pants, and Anne had twigs in her hair. Instinctively, he reached over to remove them.

"What are you doing?" she asked.

"Making you decent."

"It would've been easier if you had just pretended I was a cat."

He stopped removing leaves and traced his palm around the sweet curve of her cheek. Common sense warned that he ought to get moving. What if someone saw them? Or, worse, what if he pressed a long, slow kiss on her full lips?

In two more days, Eric would pledge his eternal devotion to a woman who desperately needed his strength. A woman he respected and cared for.

And yet...

For a fleeting moment, he allowed himself to wonder what it would be like if he were marrying Anne. If instead of loyalty and tenderness, he felt magic sparkling through his veins?

He caught himself up short. What on earth was wrong with him? He hadn't seen Anne for five years. Despite their old acquaintance, they scarcely knew each other. California had been a wonderful adventure that he remembered with wistful nostalgia, but it had nothing to do with his world now.

Drawing his hand away from Anne, he restrained

the urge to dust some pollen off the curving lines of her jacket. He ignored the chill that crept over him at the loss of contact.

"First things first," he said. "Why were you following me?"

"Mrs. Knox ordered me to spy on you." Standing up, she began plucking residue from her suit.

"Why?" Eric got stiffly to his feet.

"She's got some idea that women are trying to steal you." Anne shook her head. "Can you imagine? Who would do a dim-witted thing like that?"

He chose not to respond to her teasing. "Caro's mother ordered you to make sure I don't run off with some other woman?"

"That's right."

"Where on earth did she get that idea?"

She shrugged. "Your mother planted some gossip about your stepsister, Bianca."

Gossip about Bianca? He couldn't imagine what his mother might have said; no doubt Mrs. Knox had simply misunderstood. Still, he found it hard to account for her sending Anne—of all people!—to keep tabs on him.

"Are you saying that you're supposed to guard my honor?" Under the circumstances, Eric couldn't help finding the idea amusing.

"Ridiculous, huh?" she said. "Also, Genevieve saw you arguing with Caroline, not that it's any of my business. She's worried that things might unravel."

"We're all a bit high-strung over this wedding," he said. "Something less splashy might have been a good idea. Still, we have to meet people's expectations."

"By the way," Anne said, "congratulations."

"On what?"

"Your forthcoming nuptials. Also your magazine. You've done well."

Her good wishes appeared to be genuine. Most people would never be that generous. "You don't hold it against me, about the byline?"

She faced him squarely. "Did you set me up?"

"No," he said. "I honestly didn't."

"Well, you acted like a jerk anyway," she said, "but I forgive you."

"Thanks." It might be irrational, but Eric felt a burden lift from him. However little they might move in the same circles, he valued Anne's friendship. As well as her professional talents.

"By the way, why *are* you working as Genevieve's secretary?" he asked. "It's a waste of your experience."

Balancing on one foot, she removed a pump and dumped out a small cloud of debris. "I'd been freelancing for peanuts and then, two years ago, I read about an opening at *The Loop*. I was tired of my career going nowhere, so, like an idiot, I drove to Chicago for an interview."

"You wanted to work for me?" he asked in surprise.

"I was at my wits' end." She sighed. "Anyway, I showed up for my interview with your assistant editor and she said, sorry, the position was filled. She said she tried to call me but I was on the road."

Eric got a hollow sensation. He'd missed a golden opportunity, and he'd missed it because of his own impulsiveness.

"I had no idea," he said. "You would've been terrific for the job."

"I trust you hired someone good. Maybe he or she would have beaten me anyway."

Not in this lifetime. He couldn't bring himself to deceive her, even by omission. "One of my friends from prep school recommended his younger brother. He'd just graduated from journalism school and I figured I'd give him a break."

"You didn't interview competitively?" she asked.

"I had a chat with the kid, looked at his writing samples and made a snap decision. He's working this wedding, as a matter of fact."

Monty DeLong's writing was hip and confident, and the kid had the right connections among the city's elite. It had taken Eric a few months to discover what the young man lacked: thoroughness and objectivity.

Still, Eric felt a responsibility to guide the young man. Things had gone well for the past few months, until he received Gabby's phone call today. Still, he hadn't read the article yet; maybe it wasn't as hopeless as she implied.

"It was crazy for me to think we could work together anyway," Anne added.

"No, it wasn't." He jammed his hands into his pockets. "I wish I'd hired you. But how did Genevieve come into the story?"

"My car broke down the day I got here, and I couldn't afford the repairs, or a plane ticket, either." Anne removed the other shoe and emptied it. "I needed a job in a hurry, and the employment agency said she paid well. I had no idea her daughter had been your college sweetheart, and even when I found out you two were dating, well, I didn't think it would affect me. The engagement was rather sudden, wasn't it?''

He preferred to avoid that topic. ''Does she really expect you to stick to me for the next two days?''

''Like glue, she said.''

''Even while I'm jogging?'' He tried to picture Anne loping after him in her beige suit and pumps.

''Is that what you're going to do now?''

''I exercise twice a day,'' he said. ''To work off the nervous energy.''

''You and Caroline can't figure out a better way?'' She bit her lip in mock embarrassment. ''Oh, excuse me! Did I say that? Shame on me!''

He refrained from asking how she worked off *her* energy. Thinking about that topic was putting a strain even on his pleated pants. ''You never were one to beat around the bush.''

''Except when I'm being a cat.'' She moved toward the path. ''I will skip the jog, though, if you don't mind. I've got a stack of thank-you notes to write for Caroline.''

He was faintly displeased to learn his bride didn't write her own thank-you notes. Then he remembered that he wasn't writing very many such letters himself, so he had no right to criticize.

''Genevieve did say to stick like glue. You should at least come in and watch me change,'' he joked.

''Duty has its limits.''

''Suppose I open the cottage door and some ravening female abducts me?'' He tried to look innocent, and knew he was failing miserably.

''Nobody ever made Eric Bellamy do anything he didn't want to do,'' Anne said briskly. ''And since my mission is to ensure that your groomly jitters don't lead you astray, the less time I spend alone with you, the better. See you at the rehearsal tonight.''

Eric might have argued, if he hadn't needed to call the office and straighten out Monty's mess. Besides, as Anne pointed out, his capacity for resisting temptation was a bit shaky.

Taking a firm grip on his inclinations, he gave her a casual salute and watched her walk away.

IT WAS THE FIRST TIME in two years that Anne had neglected her duties. If she weren't going to stay with Eric, she ought to return to Genevieve and assist at the garden party.

Not that she'd been fibbing about the thank-you notes, but they could be handled next week. She'd left because she wanted solitude to absorb her impressions and bring her emotions in line. Also to change out of this rumpled suit.

She decided to repair to her small room adjoining Genevieve and Hainsworth's suite, on the hotel's third floor. Maybe she would take a bath long enough to drown the unwanted sensations raging through her body.

How rotten of Eric to have grown even better looking over the years! His face was more strongly defined, his eyes deeper and darker, and when he'd touched her, she'd felt the tenderness in his hands.

How could he have this effect on her, when she knew he was marrying someone else? Someone with whom he'd no doubt gained the experience that made him such an alluring adult?

As she slipped past the gazebo and over the bridge

at the mouth of the pond, Anne was grateful not to catch sight of Caroline. Eric had never truly belonged to Anne, so she had no reason to resent the other woman. She did wish Genevieve's daughter would act a little more gracious toward the hired help, though.

Well, this weekend would be over soon enough. Two more days. The time would vanish before she realized it.

When she reached the side of the hotel, Anne swung toward the front, avoiding the garden party. She didn't want the guests, or her boss, to observe her flustered state.

As she rounded the corner, the sound of shouting drew her attention to the front gate a short distance down the driveway. A TV news crew stood next to their van, arguing heatedly with the hotel's security chief.

At that moment, a sports car pulled up nearby. Out hopped a young man with longish blond hair. Waving a notebook, he began making demands of his own.

Her experience as a reporter made Anne sympathize with the desire to get a story. However, this was hardly meaningful journalism. These people were trying to rip off Eric's and Caroline's private lives to make a buck, and that side of the news business repelled her.

She supposed she must have lost touch with the times. These days, readers wanted the sizzle, not the steak. She hoped that when she finally got back into the profession, she could find a way to deliver both.

With a metallic scrape, the front gates swung open, separating the two wrought-iron swans that formed a heart symbol. The blond fellow jumped into his car and gunned his way through.

He zoomed past Anne, coming so close she took a cautionary step backward. The man didn't even tap his brakes.

At the front portico, he screeched to a halt. Emerging with a bound, he tossed his keys and his leather bag to the head porter.

"Montcrief DeLong with *The Loop*," he called as he went up the steps. "Take care of these, and get me checked in, pronto! You can bring my key around to the party."

"Sir, I'm afraid my duties don't include—"

"I haven't got time for a discussion! I've got a job to do!" A frown elongated the young man's face. "I work for Eric Bellamy, in case you hadn't figured that out. Now let's both do the jobs we're being paid for, okay?"

Without noticing Anne, let alone apologizing for nearly running her over, the fellow cut through the main building toward the garden. He obviously took it for granted that his orders would be obeyed.

The porter's exasperated expression was priceless. Anne wished she could see a shot of *that* in *The Loop*.

"Charming fellow," she observed dryly.

The porter hefted the suitcase, which bore a prominently placed designer logo. "Are you all right, miss? He nearly hit you."

"My ego's a little bruised, that's all," she said. "Are you going to check him in?"

"Why, of course," said the porter. "The staff at Swan's Folly bends over backward to accommodate our guests." He heaved an exaggerated sigh. "It's too bad about the mix-up in the reservations, though.''

''What mix-up?''

''It seems the clerk accidentally gave Mr. De-Long's room to another guest, or he's going to when I suggest it,'' the man said. ''We've had a couple of people arrive without reservations who were put on a waiting list. I'm sure one of them could use it.''

''He's got to sleep somewhere,'' she pointed out.

''We have a little room we save for emergencies, down in the basement near the kitchen,'' said the porter. ''Right under the billiards room. Gets a bit loud, what with guests playing pool till late, and then the food deliveries arrive so early. But I'm sure the desk will provide complimentary earplugs.''

He held the door for Anne. As she went through, she thought she detected the faint sound of humming.

ERIC STRETCHED his legs along the leather cushions on the sofa and watched late-afternoon light stream through the windows of Ivy Cottage. Despite the luxury of a cathedral ceiling and a private fireplace, he felt not the least bit relaxed as he listened on his cell phone.

The way his traffic editor laid it out, the situation with Monty's article was worse than Eric had realized. The kid had outdone himself this time.

After noticing a discrepancy in Monty's descriptions of a rent-a-date service, Gabby had called the head of the company to sort it out. The woman denied saying some of the quotes and threatened to call her lawyer about the implication that she was running a thinly disguised brothel.

''It throws the whole story into doubt,'' Gabby

told him. "Someone needs to double-check the other people he interviewed, including the rival dating service and all the individuals who were quoted. Plus, under the circumstances, I recommend we get some outside comment to put things into perspective. Maybe a sociologist from the university."

Eric rubbed his temple, which was starting to throb. "What's the deadline on this?"

"We need the re-write by Monday," said the traffic editor. "And I'm talking first thing in the morning. If my coffee has time to get cold, the article's late."

To catch people in their offices, the calls would have to be made today and tomorrow. Mentally, Eric reviewed the members of his staff who might be available.

The Loop relied mostly on freelancers, keeping only a few full-time writers. One of those was Monty himself.

Why had Eric ever been foolish enough to hire such a novice? Because, he admitted silently, the kid matched the suave profile of young Chicagoans projected by *The Loop*. On the surface, he had seemed a perfect fit.

"What about Maureen?" he asked, citing the staff's senior writer.

"You gave her a long weekend off, remember? She's incommunicado with her latest boyfriend."

"Call her anyway."

"I'm not kidding about the incommunicado bit. Her cell phone and pager are sitting right on her desk. I think they went sailing and plan to sleep on the boat."

"How about Phil?" His name came next on the masthead.

"His wife's having a baby. She went into labor an hour ago. Don't even ask about Trevor. You sent him to Atlanta on assignment, remember?"

Beverly, the assistant editor, lay in the hospital recovering from surgery, Eric knew. Fate must be conspiring against him. Only one qualified person remained at the magazine offices. "I know you're not exactly a reporter, but—"

"I'm an even worse writer," Gabby interjected. "Plus, with that woman threatening to call her attorney, I wouldn't touch this one with a ten-foot pole. I'm afraid it's your headache, Mr. Publisher and Editor-in-Chief."

Literally a headache, Eric reflected, pressing his thumb into his temple. "Maybe it's not as bad as it sounds. E-mail me the story and your notes, and I'll make the calls."

"I knew I could count on you," she drawled, and signed off.

He'd already hooked up his laptop computer to the cottage's telephone line. He'd planned to access the latest news on the Internet, not conduct business, but that was life in the publishing world.

Caroline would be upset if he disappeared for most of tomorrow. However, there were no official activities slated on Friday until the bachelor and bachelorette parties in the evening. Eric hoped he could whip this thing out of the way by then, at least.

As for Caro's moods, he'd had plenty of experience in dealing with those. He thanked his stars that they weren't staying in the same unit.

It had seemed like a waste of space, for him to

stay solo in Ivy Cottage with its loft-style bedroom, large living room and cozy dining area. Now he was grateful that he had plenty of room for a temporary office.

Maybe it wouldn't be so bad, he told himself as he went upstairs to change for his afternoon jog. He'd make some quick calls tomorrow morning and apply his lightning talents to polishing up Monty's story. Without distractions, he might be able to finish by mid-afternoon.

Eric yanked off his suit and tossed it over a chair. From a drawer, he pulled one of several sets of exercise clothes.

As soon as he returned from his honeymoon— which reminded him that he ought to ask Caroline where they were going—he was going to call Monty on the carpet. Give that young pup one more chance to get his act together, and make it clear he would tolerate no more irresponsibility.

Then Eric remembered that he still had to mend this afternoon's disagreement with Caro. They'd be on display tonight, with both their families gathered.

A man could always work things out, though, if he took the right approach. And if he could manage to ignore the memory of Anne's soft shape beneath him in the grass, and the warmth of her laughter, and the sound of her voice saying, *You acted like a jerk...but I forgive you.*

Chapter Four

So much for collecting her thoughts and recovering her equanimity, Anne thought. As she nibbled her meal and listened to conversations swirling around her at the rehearsal dinner, she felt as much at sea as she had this afternoon.

The wedding party had taken over the hotel restaurant. Most of the participants were scattered about at tables, but the bride's and groom's families sat, rather awkwardly, at a long table set on a dais.

In the center of the table, clearly visible from where Anne sat with Genevieve near one end, the happy couple basked in the limelight. They were larger than life, the golden-haired princess and her darkly handsome prince.

The bride's pink cocktail dress, although a bit fussy, shouted "Expensive!" from the self-covered buttons to the hand-sewn ruffles. By contrast, Anne's pale green sheath and matching jacket had come off the rack at a discount store.

She had to admit, she couldn't see herself ever being so glamorous or so elegant. Anne, preening in the spotlight? Hardly!

When she wasn't crouching in bushes and picking

twigs out of her hair, she preferred to keep a low profile, whether as Genevieve's assistant or as a journalist. Reporting meant observing people quietly, letting them reveal themselves. The ability to let others take center stage was essential.

You'd have been terrific for the job. Had Eric meant that? Should Anne consider applying to him for a position after leaving Genevieve's employment?

She'd read a few issues of *The Loop* and been impressed by its fresh graphics and lively style. Despite their cleverness, however, the articles rarely delved below the surface.

Would Eric be willing to consider taking a different approach from time to time? And could Anne bear the frustration of working with him when he belonged to someone else?

"This is Caro's special moment." Genevieve eyed her daughter. "I hope she makes the most of it. A woman never has quite the same glow again, after her wedding."

"Mom!" The protest came from Winnie, Caroline's younger sister and maid of honor, who sat across from her mother. "You sound so old-fashioned! I mean, honestly, nobody's wedding night makes much difference these days!"

"I didn't mean *that*," said Genevieve. "Although I hardly think you should be discussing such matters."

"Oh, everybody knows everything these days!" The twenty-year-old emphasized her point by wiggling lustily inside her laced-up bustier. From the amount of motion, Anne could tell she wasn't wearing a bra.

So, apparently, could the youngest of the ushers, twenty-three-year-old Kevin, who was sitting nearby. He dropped his fork onto his plate with a clink and, reaching for it, bumped his water glass hard enough to slop liquid onto the tablecloth. Winnie giggled.

Hainsworth Knox glowered across the table. "Winnifred!" When he addressed his daughter formally, it was not a good sign. "This is an inappropriate way to behave, and I do not approve of your choice of clothing."

Winnie stared down at her cleavage. "What's wrong with it? Kevin, don't you think I look okay?"

His Adam's apple wobbled. "Uh, sure."

"Did you see the shocked look Reverend Lovejoy gave you at the rehearsal?" Hainsworth indicated the minister's ramrod-straight figure at the far end of the dais. "I'm sure he found your outfit disrespectful, and so do I."

Genevieve laid one hand on her husband's coat sleeve. "You're quite right, dear. Thank you."

Hainsworth stared at his wife in astonishment. Usually, she greeted his comments with either silence or an acid response.

Facing a united front from her parents, Winnie caved in. "Maybe tomorrow I'll wear one of those fancy velvet dresses that Lizzie gave us. Anne, have you seen the samples she brought from her dress shop?"

"They're stunning, aren't they?" Genevieve said. "Lizzie—Elizabeth Muldoon—was Caro's roommate in college, you know. I wasn't sure I was doing the right thing when I invested in her store, but it's booming."

"I was dubious myself, but you showed good

judgment," said Hainsworth. "I'm proud of you, dear."

The couple smiled shyly at each other, like a pair of teenagers on a first date. Anne hoped once again that their daughter's wedding was reawakening memories of their own romantic courtship.

During the past two years, she'd watched her fearsome boss display more and more signs of vulnerability. She hoped Genevieve wasn't becoming dotty like Nana. A little mellowing wouldn't hurt, though.

Kevin's gaze kept straying to Winnie's breasts. Each slip would be followed by much fidgeting and enough throat clearing to alarm an ear, nose and throat specialist.

Finally he arrived at a topic of conversation. "So," he said to Anne, "the White Sox are looking better this year, don't you think?"

"I'm still something of a California Angels fan," she admitted.

"The Angels?" Astonishment replaced his restlessness. "Are you kidding? They couldn't hit a ball if it came up and blew them a raspberry!"

The friendly quarrel that followed was exactly what Anne needed to take her mind off the wedding. She even developed enough appetite to clean her plate.

ERIC STARED AT his dessert and tried to remember what he'd just consumed for dinner.

He also wondered why whoever had selected the menu had chosen to end it with something pink and frothy instead of an apple tart or a scoop of doublechunk chocolate ice cream. It was, as he often pointed out to his readers, possible to be up-to-the-minute without losing sight of basic values. Such as the fact that food was supposed to be edible.

Did everything have to match the pink-and-white colors of the wedding decor? Not only was the dessert pink, but the hotel's ballet-themed restaurant had been strung with crepe paper in the approved hues. It looked painfully out of place.

Eric scolded himself for being so critical. It wasn't really the food or the decorations that were troubling him.

It was the fact that he'd noticed how, at the end of the long table, Anne's eyes sparkled as she chatted with his half brother Kevin. What was she saying to make the young man so animated? Why was he studying her with the rapt interest he usually reserved for sports?

Eric experienced a pang, not of jealousy but of envy, at Kevin's freedom to enjoy her company. Close enough to inhale her fragrance.

Okay, he was jealous, too, he admitted. It was unfair that she should find that young rogue so fascinating. What *were* they talking about?

"Darling," said Caro, startling him. "If you stare at my mother any harder, she might burst into flames." Genevieve was sitting with Anne, which explained the fortunate mistake.

"I was just…thinking how handsome she looks at her age. As you will, when you grow older." It was blatant flattery and subterfuge, and Eric should have been ashamed. Instead, he was grateful for the chance to buy peace.

Although neither referred to their earlier quarrel, Caro had kept her emotional distance all evening. He couldn't blame her; preoccupied by thoughts of the mess Monty had made, he wasn't very good company.

"You won't be disgusted, when I have wrinkles and gray hair?" she asked earnestly.

Eric let his gaze linger on the vision beside him. In a pink frock, with her hair upswept and a pair of diamonds sparkling in her ears, Caroline looked positively regal.

"You'll be gorgeous at any age. By the way, have I mentioned how beautiful you look tonight?" he asked.

She thawed slightly. "Thank you." And waited expectantly for more.

Under normal circumstances, compliments came easily to Eric. Tonight, however, he couldn't focus. "The rehearsal went well, don't you think?" was the best he could manage.

"You mean aside from your stepsister oversleeping her nap and inconveniencing everyone?" A dangerous note crept into Caroline's voice, a reminder that it was he who had insisted on including Bianca in the wedding party.

"She has jet lag." And a baby that nobody except Eric knew belonged to his brother, Neill. Even Neill himself hadn't figured it out, the numbskull. "Also, she's dealing with some problems I'm not free to talk about."

"You know, dearest, it isn't necessary to take responsibility for your entire family." Caro dabbed her lips with a cloth napkin. "They rely on you way too much to play peacemaker. You're going to be my family now. My next of kin. My husband. *Those* are the responsibilities you should take seriously."

"And you think I don't?"

She blinked, as if she hadn't expected such a direct response. "I only meant that your mind seems to be wandering."

He cupped his hand over hers. "You're right. I apologize."

"Let's pretend the weekend begins now," said his bride-to-be.

"Agreed." He started to pat her hand, and stopped himself. Why was he behaving like a fond uncle? "Since we're going to be next of kin, I think it's time we shared more of our lives."

"Oh?" She raised one shapely eyebrow. "I thought we shared everything already."

"Not entirely," he said. "I mean, about work."

Monty's story, when it arrived via E-mail, had turned out to be a bigger train wreck than Eric expected. According to Gabby's notes, there were questions about almost every aspect.

The man had painted the dating service's female clients as virtually prostitutes. He'd inserted damning quotes from a vice detective, quotes that Gabby believed had been taken from an unrelated interview concerning a resurgence of organized crime in Chicago.

Under normal circumstances, Eric would have edited the article himself and caught the problems earlier. Due to the preparations for his wedding, however, he'd entrusted it to his assistant editor, who, in retrospect, he could see must have been distracted by her thyroid problems.

He wasn't sure he could fix it in such limited time. If only he had another writer to help him, someone reliable and hard-driving and thorough.

Anne. He needed Anne.

But he didn't have her. So he would have to spend all day tomorrow working like a dog, and that wasn't going to improve his standing with Caro.

Surely if she understood the problem, though, she would be supportive. Because she cared about him. And because he'd come to respect her intelligence, even if she hadn't chosen to pursue a career.

Married people relied on each other in difficult times. He had no business treating Caroline like a china doll. "For instance," he said. "We're having a problem with a potentially libelous article."

"I wouldn't know anything about that!" She fluttered her hand. "What you need is a lawyer."

"I prefer to prevent the libel from getting into print in the first place," he said. "I've only got tomorrow to fix it."

"Tomorrow?" She frowned. "Surely you're joking!"

"I wish I were."

"Why you?" she demanded. "Let one of your staff take care of it. It's your wedding weekend!"

Keep cool, he ordered himself. *She's under pressure, too, with all these people staring and all these arrangements to supervise.* "Our time together means a great deal, but we're partners now. There are occasions when we have to help each other."

"You can hardly expect me to turn into Lois Lane! Although I did always think I'd be a good journalist if I turned my hand to it."

"That's not what I meant." He smiled, a bit stiffly. "I was referring to needing your emotional support. Your understanding that I have to spend most of tomorrow working."

"This is what you mean by sharing our lives?"

As Caro's voice rose, heads turned toward them. "That I'm supposed to twiddle my thumbs while you ignore me?"

With a sinking sensation, Eric reflected that they'd battled over this issue before. And broken up over it, too.

In their younger years, he'd found Caroline's insatiable need for attention to be draining, until he learned that it stemmed from her dread of being abandoned. Also, this past year, since the announcement of their engagement, she'd seemed calmer and more mature.

Surely this regression was only temporary. "The circumstances are unusual," he told her quietly. "Normally I'd have caught the mistakes myself, but—"

"Oh, look!" Caro waved at a man entering the restaurant. "There's that darling Monty! You can have him do the work."

Without thinking, Eric lowered his head to tap his forehead against the table, a gesture he used half-humorously at work to indicate frustration. He remembered, too late, that his dessert was still sitting there, and came up with a faceful of pink trifle.

His fiancée drew back. "Wipe that off!"

Feeling foolish, he scrubbed himself with his napkin. "I can't have Monty make the corrections because he's the one who screwed up in the first place."

"All the more reason!" said Caroline. "Yoo-hoo! Monty!"

"There you are!" The young reporter thrust his way between packed tables, knocking into people without apology. His long blond hair floated into

Petsy's face, and she gave him a disgusted grimace. "Eric, you've simply got to get my room changed. They've put me in this horrible little hole under the billiards room, and it stinks from the kitchen!"

"Monty, we need you to rewrite some article or other," Caroline said.

"Caro!" Eric protested.

"But don't you see?" she replied. "I've solved your problem!"

"How can I do a rewrite when I can't think straight?" sniffed the reporter. "Who can work in such stifling accommodations?"

"Your job is to cover the wedding," Eric said. "And you will do that, regardless of where you're sleeping. Furthermore, this dinner isn't one of the functions you were invited to cover."

"Very well, I'm leaving. Did you know you have pink goo on your face?" asked Monty. As he whisked away, Eric took another swipe at his nose with the napkin.

"Now you've ticked him off," Caroline said. "I wouldn't be surprised if he put it in his wedding write-up, how you look with that stuff on your face!"

"If he does, I'll edit it out."

"You'd censor his work?" she said. "Eric, that's not right. In fact, I think you should leave his article alone, the one you're planning to tinker with. There is such a thing as artistic freedom, you know!"

If he answered, Eric knew he might say something he would regret. Instead, he got to his feet, struggling to find a polite exit line. Nothing clever came to him, so, before the silence lengthened, he said a rather abrupt "Excuse me," pushed his chair back and marched out of the restaurant.

"I NEED A DRINK," said Genevieve as the guests began to disperse. It was the first comment she'd made since Eric left in a huff.

After Caroline fled to her room in tears, Hainsworth went upstairs to calm his daughter. Genevieve was, obviously, in no shape to calm anyone.

Anne didn't consider alcohol a helpful approach, but she wasn't Genevieve's mother. Not that her employer's real mother, Nana, could be relied upon to counsel moderation. Nana had swung past their table a few minutes ago in a cloud of lavender, proclaiming that she simply had to dance and that her public awaited.

The bar, which at Swan's Folly was dubbed the Cygnet Club, lay directly across the corridor from the restaurant. Anne followed her boss there, trying not to show the mixed feelings raging inside.

Why were Eric and Caroline fighting? This wasn't how couples in love were supposed to act.

Was she being middle-class and naive to think society hotshots married for reasons of the heart? For months, Anne had heard what a perfect match this was, how gorgeous they were, how they would reign over society. Nothing about love.

Yet love *did* matter to people of their station. It had certainly mattered to Genevieve when she'd married a lowly hotel employee, Anne reflected as they took seats at a small table.

That had been nearly thirty years ago, though. Her boss and Hainsworth slept in separate bedrooms now and, until this weekend, had interacted with all the warmth of two corporate executives.

Genevieve ordered a drink for herself and a Shirley Temple for her assistant, whom she knew didn't drink alcohol. The older woman proceeded to pop a pill.

"Are you sure that's wise?" Before her employer took offense, Anne explained, "That isn't a tranquilizer, is it? It could be deadly, mixed with alcohol."

"No, it's one of those whatchamacallits for my blood pressure," her employer shouted over the piano music. "Oh, dear, does my mother have to do that?"

To the amusement of the other guests, Nana was creating a swirl of color and rhythm on the dance floor, keeping time to the jazzy rhythms of Gershwin. One dark-haired bridesmaid, standing beside a pillar, smiled with encouragement.

"That's Elizabeth Muldoon. I wonder where her fiancé went?" Genevieve asked. "I hope he didn't walk out, like Eric. Oh, dear, this wedding simply must take place. Caro's nearly past her prime, you know."

"Past her prime?" Anne repeated. "She's only twenty-eight."

"Women don't age well," said her boss. "Look at my mother, for instance. Oh, no. Please *don't* look at her!"

The octogenarian, carried away by the joy of the moment, had mounted the bar and was dancing with hands on hips, Irish-style. The piano player stopped in alarm, but the silence didn't inhibit the rapid *slap-slap* of Nana's slippers as she threw herself into a solo production of Riverdance.

One of the ushers, Kevin's older brother, Joe, scooped Nana from her perilous perch and swung her down to the floor. The feisty lady responded by giving him a big kiss.

Then, beaming with satisfaction, she resumed her dancing on terra firma. Other members of the wedding party trickled into the Cygnet Club and some of them joined Nana on the floor.

"Goodness, this place is getting crowded," grumbled Genevieve. "You'd think people had nowhere else to go."

"I'm not sure that they do," Anne said.

Her boss folded her arms. "That's the problem with having guests for the weekend, isn't it? You simply can't get away from them." Her expression brightened as Hainsworth came into the room. And dimmed when he sat with some friends at another table.

Before Anne could propose that they join him, all heads except Nana's turned. Eric stood in the doorway.

Refusing to meet anyone's eye, he headed for a table in the back. Anne tensed, wondering what Genevieve would do. What could any mother do under the circumstances, though, but watch and worry?

A moment later, Lizzie joined Eric at his table. Although he kept his face turned away, the dark-haired bridesmaid began talking rapidly and patting his wrist.

"I knew it!" Genevieve smacked her glass onto the table. "The minute he's alone, that girl is after him!"

"I beg your pardon?" Anne thought it was Bianca who was supposed to be chasing Eric.

"Elizabeth Muldoon has had a crush on that man since college," Genevieve said fiercely.

"But she's Caroline's friend!"

"Mark my words, she'd snap him up in a minute."

Eric drew female attention as naturally as breathing, Anne reflected. Generally, he responded with friendship and polite interest, nothing more.

When they'd worked together, she'd heard other women at the office complain because he declined to hop into their beds. Knowing that he didn't play around was one of the reasons that she'd let down her guard, that night when they slept together.

His refusal to stand up to their editor the next day still rankled. But since he mentioned it, Anne could see now that it was she who dumped him and not the other way around.

"You're worrying for nothing," she said. "Eric's not an alley cat, and if he didn't want to marry your daughter, he wouldn't have asked her. Why would he go for another woman at a time like this?"

Genevieve tapped her fingers on the table. "Because he's vulnerable. There are times when men can hardly help themselves. He could be led astray, believe me."

The woman's gaze fixed on Hainsworth, who was laughing with his friends. Had he done something to alienate his wife? Anne wondered. If so, it must have happened before she came to work there.

Suddenly Genevieve stared around her in distress. "I don't believe it! Where did they go?"

"Who?" Anne noticed the empty table where Eric and Lizzie had been sitting. "I'm sure they're around."

Her employer grabbed her shoulder. "You're supposed to watch him!"

"I can't dog his every step," Anne returned. "How would it have looked if I'd stood up and followed on his heels when he left the restaurant?"

"Well, go and check on him!" Genevieve commanded. "Take a peek in his cottage and make sure he's there—alone."

Anne's stomach clenched. She wasn't afraid to stroll around the hotel grounds at night, even though Eric's cottage was located some distance from the main building. But to enter his masculine lair alone, when he'd been drinking and they were both too tired to keep their guard up, seemed like asking for trouble.

She knew the dark invitation in his eyes, and the teasing tilt of his head, and the heady male scent of him. What woman could help but experience a physical response to the sexiest man she's ever met?

"That might not be a good idea." When Genevieve's jaw set and her eyes narrowed, Anne added, "What excuse could I give for barging in?"

"Say I asked you to look for my daughter."

"I thought she was in her room." Caroline was occupying the bridal suite solo until Saturday night.

"How would he know whether she's there?" demanded Genevieve. "Unless he's there with her, in which case he won't be at his cottage, will he?"

Anne couldn't refute the logic. Instead, she said, "What if Lizzie or someone else is with him?"

"Offer to walk her home," Mrs. Knox ground out between clenched teeth. "If she refuses, rip her hair out by the roots."

With a heavy heart, Anne stood up. Although she didn't want to run this errand, she could hardly admit her own prior relationship with Eric, at this late date.

Besides, nothing would happen. Anne's sense of loyalty to her employer ran deep. And while Eric might indulge in some light flirting, she didn't believe he would betray his fiancée.

"All right," she said. "Do you want me to pop into your suite and fill you in when I get back?" Anne's small room connected to Genevieve and Hainsworth's sitting room, although it also had an exit to the hallway.

Genevieve stifled a yawn. "No, I'm sleepy. I know I can trust you to take care of things."

"Yes," Anne said. "You can."

ERIC TOSSED HIS COAT and tie across the back of a chair. Even in this large cottage, he felt like a caged tiger.

He wanted to get on with his work, but he could hardly phone Monty's sources at this hour. Nearly eleven o'clock, by the mantel clock.

What he needed was someone to sound off to. Not about Caroline; despite his frustration, he owed her his discretion. But about incompetent kid reporters, and odd-tasting pink desserts, and even dear old friends who believed they could counsel and reassure him.

Lizzie had a natural inclination to rescue people that reminded him of his stepbrother Joe, the fireman. But Eric could only be rescued by someone able to put any situation into perspective with the crack of her wit, someone whose green eyes had sparkled much too brightly at another man tonight.

Anne. That was who he needed. Outspoken, honest, warm and touchable Anne.

His longing astonished him. After all these years,

he'd believed he was cured. Heck, he hadn't even acknowledged until now that there was anything to be cured of.

The way she made love was different from the few other women he'd slept with. He'd gotten lost in her sensuality and her unrestrained eagerness. She'd held nothing back, and, as a result, neither had he.

He'd mourned the loss of her friendship for months. He'd tortured himself, wishing they could do things over, that he could have a second chance.

Now the thought of her soothed Eric's soul. Thank goodness he'd come back to his cottage while she was still occupied with Genevieve. There was no chance of running into her tonight, and by tomorrow he would have himself under control.

He would find a way to soothe Caroline. Sure, she'd said some silly things tonight, but how was a sheltered heiress supposed to understand the realities of his profession?

Unworking the top buttons of his shirt, Eric let the evening air draw the heat from his skin. He felt too restless to go to sleep yet. Maybe he should drop in on Neill and reminisce about the good old days when they and Mom and Dad had been a real family.

Two sharp knocks startled him. Perhaps his brother had beaten him to the punch, or one of the other groomsmen had come in search of a nightcap. It didn't matter who it was; Eric would be grateful for anyone to take his mind off the past.

"Come on in," he drawled as he opened the door. Then his heart performed a couple of loop-de-loops.

There she stood, temptation itself, looking more

flustered than he'd ever seen her. Flushed cheeks, glittering eyes, full lips.

The woman of his dreams. Not the one he had promised to marry, but the one he ached to take to his bed.

Indeed, that he'd slept with Dietrich during their marriage at all, for that matter.

He wanted all his money. Not because he had promised to pay it, but for the sake of his son, his heir.

Chapter Five

Anne had spent the brief walk to the cottage preparing for this moment. She was going to make sure no unauthorized females were hanging around, say something offhand about her duties as a spy and leave. Depart. Amscray. Before she fell under Eric's spell.

But even the best laid plans come unglued. Because there Eric stood, dangerously handsome, his shirt open and his hair tousled. She couldn't get a word out.

"Anne! Come in!"

Her jaw moved stiffly. "You're alone, right?" she mumbled.

He held the door wider.

"I, uh—" *Brilliant start, Anne.* She tried again. "You're not, uh—I mean, my boss asked—" This was getting her nowhere. "I came to throw Lizzie out on her tush—to save you for Caro. I'll go now."

Laughter rolled from his throat. "I get the picture. Please don't leave yet."

Anne clasped her hands in front of her like a little girl. "Eric, I don't want to..." She cleared her throat.

"I don't want to get in the middle of—whatever. You need to be with Caroline, not me."

His jaw worked and then, to her relief, he yielded. "You're right."

"You could come back to the hotel and see her," she offered. Although that would require spending a few minutes in each others' company while they walked, it was for a good cause.

"The problem isn't tonight, it's tomorrow." He considered briefly before adding, "I could spend a lot more time with Caro if you'll help me."

"What kind of help did you have in mind?"

"Come in and I'll tell you."

Glancing into the cottage, she got the impression of airy space and comfortable furnishings—and she found it almost unbearably enticing. "I'd prefer to stay out here."

"Is that necessary?" He cocked an eyebrow. "I'm not going to jump on you twice in one day. Besides, I have to make an admission of stupidity, and it isn't the sort of thing I like to bandy about in public."

"In public?" The wooded area was empty, although a rustling in the trees hinted at the presence of miscellaneous small animals. "You think the squirrels might rat on you?"

"Not the squirrels," he said, "but you never know when you'll run across a clever cat. And I'd very much like to talk to this one."

Anne's resistance melted. Besides, she wasn't accomplishing anything by standing on the doorstep like a kid on Halloween. Might as well go inside for her trick, or her treat.

"Okay. Make it brief." She followed him into the softly lit room.

"Does 'brief' leave room for a drink?" He indicated a wet bar and refrigerator.

"I don't drink," she said.

"Since when?"

"Since it was demonstrated to me that half a bottle of wine could cloud my judgment," she said. "Don't take that personally."

"I'll try not to." He closed the door behind her. At her questioning glance, he explained, "I wouldn't want to let in any fireflies."

"Why not? They'd add a charming touch. Little magic lights, twinkling near the ceiling."

"They might get trapped," he said. "Magic can be fragile. I wouldn't want to risk it."

There *was* something magical about the cottage, Anne reflected, as if it came from long ago and far away. She could picture a midwinter blaze in the fireplace, and herself cuddled up with Eric on the rug, drinking hot chocolate and watching the flames. After a long day of skiing, perhaps.

Afterward, they would climb those stairs together, to the bedroom above. Giggling, brushing lightly against each other, stopping halfway up for a long kiss...

"Like it?" he asked.

"Mmm?"

"The cottage," he prompted, watching her.

Anne hoped he hadn't guessed her thoughts. "It's very romantic. I'm surprised Caroline isn't staying here with you. Or would that look bad to the family?"

"The truth is, Caro and I..." He stopped. "Sorry. I was about to be indiscreet."

About what? she wondered. "And it's not indiscreet for me to be alone with you?"

"I could hardly send a beautiful maiden trudging home alone through the swan droppings, without offering her a drink and a brief respite." He gestured toward the couch. Anne remained standing. "What's your hurry, anyway?"

"I only meant to check on you so I could reassure Genevieve."

"What does she think I'm going to do?" He slanted her an amused look. "Begin interviewing for my harem?"

"Genevieve has the idea that men are easily led astray, although I don't know why. As far as I can tell, Hainsworth hasn't given her any reason to think that." Anne nibbled at her lip before speaking again. "Now I'm the one being indiscreet."

Eric paced across the carpet. "Well, I didn't invite you inside for any nefarious purposes. I wasn't kidding about needing your help. Or about my own stupidity, either."

Anne settled onto a tapestried chair. "I'm listening."

"That admission of stupidity got your interest, did it?"

"It has a certain appeal, yes," she said.

Eric took a seat facing her. "We've got problems with an article that has to be into production on Monday. There's nobody at *The Loop* to fix it, and I don't have time."

Behind him, she noticed a laptop computer on the dining table. "You're talking about work? You need a rewrite? Just a polish or—?"

"More than that, I'm afraid." He explained about

the dating service article and Monty's potentially libelous approach. "I need someone to call the sources and recheck the quotes, and to tone down the implications about the women involved."

"Only the women?" Anne asked. "He doesn't insult the men who use those agencies?"

Eric blinked, as if she'd scored a direct hit. "You're right. It's sexist as well as libelous. Anne, that's why I need your help. I can't think clearly in the middle of all this wedding brouhahaha."

"Brouhaha," she corrected.

"What?"

"You put an extra 'ha' in there."

"That was for emphasis." With both palms, he slicked his hair back from his temples. It sprang up again, thick and rebellious. "How can I tempt you?"

"Don't even ask."

"Anne, I know being Genevieve's assistant isn't the career you hoped for," he said. "You must be planning to get back into journalism at some point. Work on this article and I'll write you a glowing recommendation."

She could use an up-to-date referral when she began job hunting this fall, Anne conceded silently. Her others were years old.

As she weighed the offer, those dark eyes burned into hers. Eric Bellamy exerted an almost hypnotic appeal, like headlights in front of a deer. Or catnip laid before a cat.

Anne reminded herself that her duty was to make sure this marriage came off. The risks involved in spending time alone with the groom were too great. "I can't do it. Too many pheromones."

His forehead creased. "Pheromones? Are those like homonyms?"

"No, they're not words that sound alike," she said, and couldn't resist adding, "Like chaste and chased."

"Or lust and lost?"

"Those don't sound alike."

"They do to me," he said wistfully. "Wait a minute. Don't pheromones have something to do with insects?"

"They use them to attract mates. According to an article I read, people give them off, too." Anne stood up, keeping a tight grip on herself. "They influence people's emotions and behavior, particularly their sexual responses. If I assisted you in your own cottage, I'd be inhaling bucketloads of yours."

"Bucketloads of my what?" Eric teased.

"Your—vibes," she said, for want of a better word. "Passionate, immoral vibes."

"Hey!" He scrambled to his feet. "I'm not going to sit here and let you slander my pheromones."

"Two minutes ago, you didn't know you had any." She took a step toward the exit, until Eric thrust himself into her path.

He ran his hands lightly along her arms, raising goose bumps. "I assure you, my pheromones have the highest moral character."

"Your pheromones are hardened seducers," she said. "Unbuttoned halfway down their chests, breathing hard, teeth parted hungrily..."

"Very hungrily," he said, and his mouth closed over hers.

Like a blurry lens that comes abruptly into focus, Anne's turmoil clarified into pure hot desire. When

Eric's tongue probed beneath her lips, she caught his shoulders and pressed upward, returning his kiss.

His arms caught her to him, pinning her hips against his, stoking her need. She felt him come alive in every cell, and herself responding, everywhere.

Anne touched Eric's roughened cheek and the vulnerable pulse of his throat. She inhaled his subtle essence and let it fill her. The sensations seared away any hope of resistance.

Against his chest, her breasts swelled and the nipples tightened beneath her blouse. When his thumb traced one of the round orbs, the fiery pressure felt almost like release.

Sheer pleasure mellowed the planes of Eric's face. He trailed kisses from her forehead down her nose, planting one on the tip. At the same time, his thumbs made lazy circles around her nipples until she thought she might burst.

"Anne, I don't know what's happening," he murmured. "When I'm with you, it's as if I'm suddenly myself. The rest of the time, I don't know who I am."

"I don't know who I am either," she admitted. "Eric, we can't do this."

"You're right." He nuzzled her throat. "We need to stop."

They stood with foreheads touching, their breathing rapid. Neither quite able to let go.

She'd been wrong to shut him out five years ago. The two of them belonged together, or they would have, if he hadn't made a commitment to someone else.

Or was she kidding herself? Anne wondered.

Maybe this was just an isolated moment. "It wouldn't last," she said abruptly.

"You mean us?"

"Yes." It took all of her strength to utter the word.

He swallowed hard. "Anne, I wish—well, Caroline needs me, and we care for each other. It's different from what you and I share, but I can't violate her trust. We couldn't build a future on a betrayal."

Anne knew he was right, but she didn't have enough self-control to stand there calmly and agree. The only thing she could do was pull free and run. So she did.

Out the door. Out of the cottage. Away from the only man in the world who made her feel fully a woman.

ERIC STOOD frozen in place. What had happened? What on earth had he been thinking?

He'd craved Anne so intensely that he'd nearly forgotten everything else. Including his wedding, and his obligations to friends and family, and, above all, how their lovemaking might affect Anne herself.

Maybe he should postpone the wedding. Shoulder the blame and the embarrassment, and send everyone home until he figured out what was going on inside him.

He wished he could think straight. What had made him behave so unfairly toward Caro, and treat Anne downright shabbily? Thank goodness she'd had the presence of mind to stop him.

Slowly, his breathing came under control. As it did, he saw that he must have been deluded when he told Anne that he only became himself when he was with her. He became someone *other* than himself, that was the problem.

Growing up at the center of a maelstrom, son of a man who left behind the emotional wreckage of wives, children and stepchildren, Eric had found his niche early. He was the one who picked up the pieces, the shoulder to cry on, the guy that others sought when they couldn't cope any longer.

It was Eric who had stood by his mother through her second divorce from Dad, and urged her to pursue her interest in art. It was Eric whom his stepsister Bianca had phoned from Rome when she found out she was pregnant by his brother.

Heck, she hadn't yet informed Neill himself, who believed that mumps had made him sterile. Eric ought to call his brother right now and tell the idiot to pull his head out of the sand.

Then he ought to call Caroline and make up with her. How could a decent man do anything less?

He reached for the cell phone. It rang, beating him to the punch, and he picked it up dubiously. "Yes?"

"Eric?" The fatherly tones made him come to attention. "Hainsworth here. Hope I'm not bothering you."

It was the first phone call he'd received from his future father-in-law. In fact, Eric couldn't remember ever exchanging more than a few words with the man. Was he about to get a tongue-lashing for tonight's incident at dinner? "Not at all, sir."

"I wanted to make sure the staff is treating you right. Does the cottage meet your needs?"

"It's fantastic. You run a tight ship here." He wondered when the polite chitchat was going to segue into something more serious.

The other man's tone remained guarded, but friendly. "I suppose you figure I'm calling about your little tiff with my daughter."

"The thought had occurred to me, sir," he said.

"Caro can be hard to handle." The older man cleared his throat. "Like her mother, she's a Thoroughbred. It's not easy to keep her happy, although you probably understand because you're something of a Thoroughbred yourself."

"I'm the son of the Pretzel King, not a Kennedy," Eric said.

"That's one of the things I admire about you," Hainsworth said. "Your down-to-earth attitude. You started your own business and made a go of it by yourself."

"Not entirely by myself. I borrowed money from my Dad."

"And paid it back, I understand. With interest."

"True." Eric wondered why the other man's praise didn't feel as if it quite fit. He *had* succeeded, piloting his magazine to a healthy circulation and several awards. Yet sometimes he felt as if he were running in place, trying to fit the image he'd created for himself.

He hadn't become a trendsetter and successful publisher by either pure instinct or pure talent. Faced with the benign neglect of his self-involved parents, he'd deliberately chosen a role for himself and achieved it, step by step, from earning honors in college to founding *The Loop*.

Others saw him as breezy and self-assured. He saw himself as a hard-working guy who had to keep proving that he deserved success.

"There have been times in my marriage that were,

well, harder than others," Hainsworth continued. "The course of true love never did run smooth, as they say."

"I know that, sir."

"Whenever things get touchy, I remind myself that Genevieve is a different sort of creature than I am. More high-strung. More sensitive. Caro's like that, too."

"She is special, sir." Eric respected the man for trying to help. He also appreciated the reminder of the qualities that had drawn him to his fiancée in the first place.

More throat clearing preceded the next statement. "Sometimes a man can't help but notice other women," Hainsworth said. "There will always be temptations, pretty faces, more easygoing temperaments. Anything worth having is worth working for, though. A go-getter like you knows that as well as anyone."

Yes, Eric did. Although marrying Caroline wasn't exactly something he'd set out to do, still, in his deck of cards, she reigned as the undisputed queen.

"Believe me, I know that Caro and I belong together," he said.

"Yes, well hang in there, son," replied his father-in-law-to-be.

"Thank you for calling."

"I'm proud to welcome you into the family."

Eric set the cell phone on the table. He no longer had the urge to phone his brother tonight. Or to call anyone else, either.

His wedding was only two days away. Then all doubts would be erased, and, with Caroline in his arms, he would never again give a thought to another woman.

The blinking cursor on the computer screen caught his attention. It reminded Eric that, while he might have pulled himself back from the brink of disaster, he still had to fix Monty's botched story.

He could hardly patch up his quarrel with Caro if he spent all day working in the cottage. Tomorrow morning, he would figure out a way to talk Anne into helping.

Strictly as a business arrangement, of course.

ANNE AWOKE ON Friday with the warm, snuggly sense of having been held in a man's arms all night. Eric's arms.

With her eyes shut, she saw him again, lying on the foldout couch in California, sunshine falling in stripes across his half-naked body. Those splendid muscles. That rumpled hair.

She inhaled his scent, part man of the world and part primitive beast. The elemental musk—or perhaps his much maligned pheromones—made her too languorous to stir. She wished he were lying next to her. She wished she could hear him say...

"Wake up and have some breakfast, sleepyhead."

Sitting bolt upright, Anne yanked the covers around her thin nightgown. Good heavens, he was here!

He stood about four feet away, Eric in the flesh. A polo shirt caressed his broad chest, while his shorts revealed firm legs.

"What on earth?"

"Room service. Personal delivery." With a grin, he set a tray on the bedside table. "I wasn't sure what you liked, so I ordered a little of everything. Shall I remove the lids, madam?''

"You should remove yourself instead!" She glared at him. "Wait a minute. I locked my door last night. How did you get in?"

"You have two doors." Removing his athletic bag from his shoulder, Eric set it on the floor and sat on the edge of the bed.

Of course, she hadn't bothered to lock the door from the Knoxes' sitting room. "You came through Genevieve's suite?" Alarm wiped away the last traces of sleep. "Did anyone see you?"

"Hainsworth's already gone downstairs. He jogged past me by the pond." Eric sniffed at the tray. "Mmm. I brought enough for myself, too. Hope you don't mind."

Anne glanced at the clock radio, half-hidden behind the tray. Five minutes past eight. "What about Mrs. Knox?"

"My future mother-in-law must still be lazing abed. Besides, she's the one who assigned you to stick to me like glue. Whenever I'm not with Caroline, of course." Judging by the amusement in his eyes, Eric was thoroughly enjoying his prank.

"Why aren't you with Caroline?"

"I have it on good authority that she never gets up before nine and then it takes her an hour to get dressed." He lifted the edge of one dome and inhaled deeply.

In her impatience, Anne could have kicked him. "So what are you doing here?"

"I'll get to that. First things first, however." He removed the metal lids from the plates and set them on a chair. The heady aroma of maple syrup, bacon, scrambled eggs and toast filled the air.

Anne, who normally arose by six and downed a bowlful of cereal, discovered a hollow pit where her stomach ought to be. "Why don't you go away and let me eat?"

"I told you, I'm hungry, too." He slanted her a grin, then reached out and fingered her cheek. "I'd forgotten how young you look in the morning. Like a teenager."

His powerful arm brushed her shoulder. Tingles of longing sprang to life. "The last time you saw me this way, I practically *was* a teenager."

"We were just kids then, weren't we?" he said.

"Wet behind the ears." She deliberately injected a note of sarcasm in her statement, to put some emotional distance between them.

He must have gotten the point, because he shifted his attention to the food. "Which plate would you like?"

"You mean I have to choose one?" If she acted stubborn, perhaps he would leave. He could always rustle up another meal downstairs.

"No, of course not. We can share everything." He trickled syrup across the pancakes, cut a wedge and offered it to her. "I'd enjoy feeding you."

"That's going to drip on the pillow!" Anne's protest halted when he inserted the forkful of pancake in her mouth.

The taste was exquisite. The warmth that spread through her, however, had less to do with maple flavoring than with the experience of being fed by this man.

"Give me that!" She snatched the fork away from him and took a bite of bacon, and then some eggs.

"Thirsty?" He handed her a steaming mug. "As I recall, you take your coffee with cream and two sugars, right?"

Anne sipped the hot brew. "This is a wonderful way to treat a woman. Too bad I know that you have an ulterior motive."

"Now, why should you think that?" He helped himself to some pancakes.

"Give me some more of that before you eat the whole thing yourself, and I'll tell you," she said.

He watched her take another bite, keeping his gaze fixed on her lips. He seemed to be savoring her reaction to the flavors almost as much as his own.

For a man, Eric had always been unusually attuned to people's moods and needs, in Anne's observation. It made him a popular friend, a good interviewer and a sensitive lover. It would also make it easy for him to manipulate others, if he chose to.

"So tell me what you think my ulterior motive is," he said.

"You didn't come here to seduce me, next door to Genevieve's suite, unless you have a death wish." Darn him, he was downing two strips of bacon at once. "Why don't you eat the toast? Put some jam on it or something."

The tip of the fork waved in midair. "You mean you want the rest of the bacon?"

"Yeah, and if you touch that last strip, I'll boot you off the bed," she said. "You can set the whole tray on my lap. I'm not an invalid."

"May I at least keep my coffee?"

"Unless I run out." Anne had no intention of going easy on this man. "Whatever you came for, you'd better spit it out fast, because in about five seconds I'm pitching you into the hall before Genevieve catches you here."

"You are one tough lady."

"That's what made me a good reporter," she said. "Well? Better explain yourself."

Setting his mug and the plate of toast aside, Eric lowered the tray onto her lap. His wrists lightly touching her thighs, he shifted the tray. "Comfortable?"

"Wildly." Wildly alert to every tiny bit of contact, she finished silently. And grateful to have the tray as a shield. "I repeat, Well?"

"I figured out what to do about Monty's story."

"Oh, did you?" She shook a packet of salt over the eggs.

"Yes. Hire you to rewrite it. Without me being anywhere on the premises, to keep you safe from the pernicious effects of my pheromones."

"I already have a job."

"Which involves watching me whenever I'm away from Caro, right?" he said. "So if I promise to spend the day with her, you'll have plenty of time to work while you guard my cottage against marauding females."

"I will *not* have plenty of time. Genevieve requires my assistance." She tried the coffee again. "That's quite nice. Do I detect a hint of cinnamon?"

"Anne, I'm serious," Eric said. "I'll pay you."

"That wouldn't be right." Anne had strict ethics about her obligations. "I can't take money from you while I'm working for Mrs. Knox."

"Okay," he conceded, "but you can take credit.

As in, a line at the end of the story that says, 'Anne Crumm contributed to this article.' It's not much, but it would help update your clip file.''

"Yes, it would.'' The prospect of calling sources, taking notes and writing them up stirred a sense of anticipation. Anne missed journalism as keenly as she might miss a close friend. Or even a lover.

"Also, if I don't spend a little time with Caroline today, she'll be hurt. So you'll be helping patch things up between her and me.''

"It's not fair to play on my loyalty to Genevieve.'' She knew she was weakening.

He forged ahead, relentlessly. "I'm a desperate man. I've given this a lot of thought, and it's the best plan for all concerned.''

He might be right. If he wasn't at the cottage with her, Anne would be safe; and he did need to spend time with Caroline.

She hadn't been kidding about Genevieve needing her, though. The woman was stressed out. Anne had to make sure her employer ate properly, took her medication and avoided drinking, especially since she was likely to indulge at tonight's bachelorette party.

"Eric, I wish I could,'' she said. "Frankly, I'd enjoy the challenge. But I owe my time to Mrs. Knox.''

"I hope you'll reconsider.'' He studied her across the tray. "You're thorough and you get to the heart of things. I intend to put that in my letter of recommendation, whether you agree to do the rewrite or not.''

His generosity, and his praise, were touching. To her surprise, Anne felt tears prick her eyes.

She genuinely liked this man. If only they'd had more time together, more of a chance to get to know each other as lovers. Or was she kidding herself? She could never fit into his world the way Caroline did.

A knock at the interior door sent her heart skittering into her throat. "Anne?" came Genevieve's throaty voice. "Dear, I simply must speak to you."

"I'll be right out!"

"No, no. I'll come in," she said, and turned the knob.

Chapter Six

The door opened slowly. "Are you decent?" Genevieve called.

"Just a minute!" Anne squeaked.

Eric gazed frantically toward the hall door but apparently decided that using it would take too much time. Instead, he dropped to the floor, grabbed his athletic bag and rolled under the bed.

A stifled sneeze testified to the fact that even the efficient staff at Swan's Folly didn't dust thoroughly beneath the ruffles. However, Anne doubted Eric planned to complain to Mr. Knox.

"Come in!"

Across the threshold advanced Genevieve's stately frame, wrapped in a golden silk bathrobe. The morning light and the lack of her customary makeup revealed an uneven complexion and bluish circles beneath the eyes.

Surely the older woman would feel the electricity in the air or pick up the scent of Eric's aftershave, Anne thought, and was relieved that her employer gave no sign of noticing anything amiss. "You're having breakfast in bed? What an excellent idea. I apologize for disturbing you so early, but there's something we must discuss."

"Yes?" she asked nervously.

The bed sagged as Genevieve lowered herself onto the edge, where Eric had been sitting until a minute ago. The springs groaned, and from beneath the bed came the strangled sounds of another sneeze.

Anne did her best to mimic the sound. "Excuse me!"

"You're not coming down with a cold, are you?" Brushing back a wing of champagne-blond hair, Genevieve frowned at her.

"I'm fine," Anne said. "Is anything wrong?"

The older woman laced and unlaced her fingers. "Yes. You see, I was so worried about the quarrel last night that I called Caro this morning. She had some disturbing news."

"Really?" Anne couldn't give a more coherent response because she'd just noticed the mug of black coffee sitting on the bedside table. How could she explain the presence of a second cup?

"When you went to Eric's cottage, did you take his word for it that he was alone, or did you go inside?" Genevieve asked.

Anne struggled to remember exactly what she'd told her boss last night. "I thought I explained that I looked through the window. Why?"

"Caroline says that late last night, Petsy's husband, Gordon, was taking a walk and he saw a woman come out of Eric's cottage."

Gordon must have seen Anne leaving. Anxiety raced through her. "Did he recognize her?"

"He assumed it was Caro, but then Petsy called

her to make sure and of course it wasn't," Genevieve said.

Like a character in an Edgar Allan Poe story, Anne imagined her guilt taking tangible form. Steam from the errant coffee cup formed a black cloud so dark she could hardly see through it, and any minute now the room would shake with Eric's heartbeat.

"How is Caroline taking it?" she asked.

"She's upset, of course. She doesn't want to lose Eric to some opportunist." The older woman frowned as she fingered a frayed spot in the bedspread. "Goodness, I'll tell Hainsworth to have this replaced at once."

Anne couldn't concentrate on bedspreads when she was awash with guilt. "Your daughter must love him very much."

"Love? Who knows?" said Genevieve. "He's a great catch, even if he does have an ego the size of the Super Bowl."

A snort from beneath the bed ended in a hacking sound. Anne clapped her napkin to her mouth. "Sorry!"

"I hate to say it about my future son-in-law, but he's too attractive for his own good," Genevieve continued. "I hope he doesn't turn out to be a philanderer like his father."

"Did Gordon give any details of the woman he saw?" Anne asked. "I mean, height, weight, that sort of thing? Were they, er, framed in the doorway together?"

"No," said her boss. "He caught a flash of light from the corner of his eye, like a door opening, and when he looked again, he saw the dark shape of a woman going down the path."

Mercifully, a reasonable explanation came to Anne. "I'll bet he saw *me!* There was a draft stirring the curtains inside the cottage, which is how I could see in. That would explain the flash of light. Then he might have spotted me hightailing it home."

She hated lying. Besides, to her, the explanation seemed transparently false. It only made her feel worse when she saw how reassured Genevieve became.

"Of course! Dear, you are a wonder! It was around the right time, too." The older woman patted her hand. "I'll call Caro and tell her."

And I, Anne thought, am going to atone by doing everything in my power to behave myself from now on. "Things often get distorted when we rely on gossip."

Getting to her feet, Genevieve stretched and retied her robe. "I feel so much better." She stopped abruptly. And stared at the mug on the side table.

Anne went hot and cold in rapid sequence. She refused to fabricate any more excuses. "I'm sorry. I should have explained right away..."

"How generous you are!" Genevieve seized the cup. "To order coffee for me, too! Nice and black, the way I like it." She took a sip. "Oh, dear, they put sugar in it. Well, I suppose it's the thought that counts."

Setting the cup down, her boss strolled into the sitting room and closed the door. As soon as she was gone, a rustling came from beneath the bed.

Eric's grimy face appeared, a dust bunny perched above one temple. "An ego the size of the Super Bowl?" he muttered.

"Hurry!" Her employer could easily return. Genevieve often remembered some key point right after leaving a room.

"How bad do I look?" Eric retrieved his gym bag. "Can I still play tennis?"

He was worried about his appearance, while she was in danger of destroying Genevieve's trust? "Tell people you were attacked by a swan!" she whispered. "Now, go!"

He whisked to the door, gave her a wink, and cleared out. The rascal! He'd enjoyed this adventure. Anne, on the other hand, had aged several years.

Sure enough, Genevieve came back into the room, mercifully oblivious to the click of the hall door. "You know what? I'm going to spend most of the day resting. I'll have the hotel send up a masseuse and a manicurist and their best hairdresser. I'm going to spoil myself rotten."

"Good for you." Anne half hoped her boss would invite her to share the royal treatment. Not so much because of the half-bitten state of her own nails and the limpness of her hair, but because it would absolutely, positively preclude any contact with Eric.

In her current emotional state, she wasn't really afraid she would succumb to Eric's charms; in fact, she was more likely to strangle him. To say that he had an ego the size of the Super Bowl wasn't an exaggeration, it was an understatement!

"When it comes to my future son-in-law, I still don't trust him." Mrs. Knox took another halfhearted sip from the coffee cup. "Or Elizabeth or Bianca, either. If it wasn't one of them that Gordon saw, I'm sure it wasn't for lack of trying on their part. Stick to him!"

"Oh, please!" Anne said. "Please don't ask me to follow him around!"

"You're right," said Genevieve.

She held her breath. A reprieve?

"You can hardly shadow him all day without attracting attention," said her boss. "Besides, he's not likely to get into trouble in public. What I want you to do is stake out his cottage. From the inside."

"Excuse me?" Anne said weakly.

Genevieve snagged a slice of toast from Eric's plate. It disappeared in three bites. "You have to find an excuse to get in there. With you on the premises, he can hardly stoop to hanky-panky. Pretend you have to polish the woodwork or something."

"They have maids for that." She gritted her teeth.

"Well, you're the clever one. How else could you get inside?"

"I could slide down the chimney like Santa Claus." *And sit in the ashes like Cinderella.*

"Hainsworth might have a suggestion." The older woman snapped her fingers. "Talk about overlooking the obvious! Caro was peeved that Eric brought his laptop computer, but he must have notes to write, E-mail to sort, that kind of thing. Since I have no need of your secretarial services today, offer yourself to him!"

Anne winced. If only Genevieve knew how close she came to doing that last night!

With every fiber of her being, she longed to argue her way out of this arrangement. She must have exhausted her capacity for creative mendacity, however, because no credible objections came to mind.

"I'm going to go call my daughter right now," said her boss. "In case you hadn't noticed, it's eight-thirty. Time for you to get dressed and go find the man. Chop-chop!''

AFTER NARROWLY winning a game of tennis against his father, Eric went indoors to work out. His place on the court was taken by Hainsworth Knox.

Although the machines at Swan's Folly paled by comparison to Eric's gym in Chicago, the room was handsomely paneled and flooded with light from tall windows. At this hour, only a handful of people came and went, and he could concentrate fully on his exercise.

Pull, push. Pull, push. Sweat beaded his torso, and Eric paused to shrug off his T-shirt. As he worked, he enjoyed the tension and release in his muscles and the occasional cool drift of air across his bare chest.

Memories of Anne teased him: strands of light-brown hair clinging lazily to her cheek; her green eyes flashing as he quarreled with her; her thigh yielding beneath his arm as he set the tray on her lap.

The blood pounded through his arteries. There wasn't enough exercise in the universe to dispel this energy.

He swung onto the stationary bike, set it to provide medium resistance, and began pedaling. Leaning forward, he strained harder and harder until he got caught up in a rhythm.

Rhythm. The rhythm method. What *were* the latest trends in contraception? he wondered. That might make an interesting article for *The Loop*. He'd find a way to work in some joke about getting there being half the fun.

Eric could certainly use a little of that kind of fun.

His entire body rebelled against his current monastic existence.

A draft on his neck interrupted his thoughts, and then tennis shoes slapped across the wooden floor. From the corner of his eye, he saw a woman stop next to him, hands on hips. Her gaze raked his bulging arms and his naked shoulders and back, which by now must be gleaming with perspiration.

Anne, here? Was he fantasizing?

"You rat," she said.

Nope, this wasn't one of *his* fantasies. Eric stopped the bike. Reaching for his T-shirt, he wiped his forehead before peeking up at her.

It was indeed Anne, dressed in white slacks and a striped knit top that provided a tantalizing glimpse of bare midriff. Her slender, nipped-in waist begged for a pair of masculine hands to encircle it. He forced himself to let it beg, unanswered.

"Is there a problem?" he said.

"Yes, there's a problem. You!" Anne must have bathed a few minutes ago, because he could smell her fresh soap. Also, thanks to static electricity, strands of hair formed a halo around her head. "How dare you put me in that position this morning!"

"I didn't put you in any position," he said. "I'm the one who had to hide, remember?"

"The massive ego strikes again." If glares were daggers, he'd be dead now. "You think the only thing that matters is that you got a little lint in your hair? For your information, I don't want to hurt Genevieve or Caroline, or lose this job, either."

"Okay, I was a little impulsive," he conceded. "But I only wanted to hire you so I could spend more time with Caro."

She released an exasperated breath. "Well, you get your wish. Genevieve has instructed me to become a stealth operative."

"Meaning what?"

"I'm supposed to volunteer my secretarial services so I can spy on your lordship at home."

Slinging the shirt around his neck, Eric grinned. "Must be my lucky day. So you're working for me after all, thanks to my mother-in-law."

"She said secretarial work," Anne growled. "She didn't mention anything about writing an article for *The Loop.*"

"If you don't, I'll have to hang around the cottage all day, working side by side with you," Eric reminded her. "You wouldn't want that, would you?"

"I'll do the rewrite," she snapped. "While you make yourself scarce. However, I'm not doing any major overhaul, not for a crummy little credit at the end. I'll verify quotes and do some polishing. No more."

"It might need more," he warned.

"Take it or leave it."

Eric didn't like ultimatums. "Once you accept this assignment, you're obliged to see it through."

"I didn't accept it! Genevieve ordered me to."

"Then tell your boss no." Hoping she wouldn't realize he was bluffing, he slid off the bike and headed out of the room. She would have to answer him quickly, he thought.

Anne stalked behind him down the short hallway. She didn't seem to notice where they were headed. "I have to help Genevieve get ready for the bachelorette party tonight. My time is limited."

"That's up to her, I'd say." Eric wasn't particularly looking forward to his own bachelor party on board the Lambert yacht. It had been his father's idea, however, so he'd agreed. "Besides, you're not her personal maid, you're her assistant."

"I wasn't talking about helping with her toilette," Anne said. "I mean making sure there are no snafus."

"With Nana floating around? I'd say snafus were the order of the day." Shouldering open the door to the men's locker room, he paused. "Well?"

"Well what?"

"Do you accept my terms for working in my cottage? You make the article publishable, no matter how completely it has to be revised."

"Your terms are total surrender!"

"Oh, hardly," he scoffed. "I'm simply asking you to do a professional job."

"I never do anything less."

"Then say yes." For emphasis, Eric spun around and went inside. Expecting to leave her with the door closed in her face. Expecting for her to pound on it and yell at him until he came out again.

He'd forgotten how single-minded Anne could be. She marched right into the men's locker room after him. "If you want to talk about doing a professional job, how did this screwed-up article get past you in the first place?"

"Anne…" A quick scan of the steamy room showed it to be empty, and Eric didn't hear any showers running. Nevertheless, if they were discovered, this was almost as compromising a situation as his being in her bedroom. "This isn't the place for a discussion."

"I'll tell you how it escaped you!" she stormed.

"You were too busy playing celebrity publisher to handle such a routine task as editing a story. When things fall apart, you think you can charm other people into picking up the pieces."

Furious, he stopped caring whether anyone came in. "You're still nursing a grudge from five years ago, aren't you? I'm not the same man I was then."

"This isn't about five years ago! This is about a mess at your magazine now, caused, I might add, by the incompetent reporter *you* hired."

"Do I hear jealousy?" He was so angry he grabbed a clean towel and headed around a corner, toward the showers. Just let her follow him there! "Because *you* weren't good enough to get the job?"

"Good enough? You yourself admitted that wasn't the case!" She came right on his heels. "My not getting hired had nothing to do with my qualifications and everything to do with your carelessness." She frowned. "No, wait, I take that back."

He stopped outside a shower curtain. "Apology accepted."

"Apology? I meant that *carelessness* is too kind a word. *Superficiality,* that's better. You hired a kid because he had connections and a glib writing style, and you were too superficial to look any further."

Her green eyes dared him to deny it. Her full lips were parted, ready to frame a retort. She was absolutely splendid, and Eric had never wanted anything as much as he wanted to kiss her.

He caught that tantalizing waistline and, off guard, Anne stumbled against him. Her bare stomach met his midsection as his mouth descended, fast and hard, to claim his prize.

She squirmed and her hands fluttered around his

shoulders in feeble protest. Not for long, though. They settled like butterflies, tentative but welcoming, as she sank deeper into the kiss.

Eric angled Anne in his arms and tasted the edge of her jaw, then the pulse of her throat. Her quivering skin and her little gasps of pleasure inflamed him.

Through a fog, he heard a noise from around the corner. The locker room door opening. Men's voices.

"You're right, Budge. That court does need resurfacing." It was Hainsworth. Caro's father. His in-law-to-be.

"Oh, my gosh," Anne gulped, close to Eric's ear.

There was no escape route. No bed to hide under, either. Lacking any other choice, he yanked her into the shower.

"My foot slipped twice!" he heard his father complain, the sound muffled by the curtain. "I'm not saying I'd have won otherwise, but it did throw me off."

"Rematch tomorrow?" Hainsworth refrained from pointing out that, since the men had undoubtedly switched sides during the game, they'd both played under the same circumstances.

Pressed tightly together in the shower stall, Eric felt Anne's heart pounding against his chest. He lowered his cheek and rested it on her hair.

"I don't know. Don't we have to show up for some kind of wedding breakfast tomorrow morning?" Budge grumbled. "All these fancy events, as if we were some kind of English nobility! I guess it appeals to the ladies. Waste of time, if you ask me."

It wasn't the most diplomatic remark, considering that Hainsworth's wife and daughter had planned the affair. Budge, however, generally said and did whatever he wanted without regard for the effect on others.

With a jolt, Eric wondered if he had more in common with his father than he'd realized. He'd never considered himself self-centered; wasn't he the one others turned to, the one who counseled his stepsister and encouraged his mother and tried to make Caro happy?

Yet Anne and Genevieve had both described him as egotistical. Hearing his father made him wonder if he shared the same blind spot to his own insensitivity.

"Oh, no!" Anne whispered, and then he heard it too, the scuffle of footsteps coming in their direction. "What if they open the curtain?"

There was only one way to ensure privacy.

Grimly, Eric turned on the water.

THE SPRAY CAUGHT Anne full in the face. She coughed and choked.

"Shhh!" Eric hissed. "They'll hear you."

How had he managed to put her in this kind of awkward situation twice in one morning? The fact that she herself had trailed him into the locker room was irrelevant. If he hadn't made her so angry, she'd never have lost awareness of her surroundings.

The man was loathesome. Outrageous. Also sexy as all get-out, and impossible to ignore.

Especially with his thick hair plastered to his head and nothing on his body except for white tennis shorts. They clung to every bulge of his hips and groin, while fingers of water outlined the contours of his well-shaped chest. The heady scent of masculine exertion mingled with his cologne.

He steered her into a corner of the stall. Grateful to be out of the spray and at least a few inches away from his hard male readiness, Anne stopped sputtering.

Only to realize that he was relishing the sight of her, wet to the skin. Her soaking knit top pasted itself to her breasts. Even with her gaze averted, she knew her taut nipples must be visible.

Why had she selected this cropped top? It hadn't been the wisest choice. Yet she knew she couldn't compare to the other women at the hotel in terms of their expensive wardrobes, their jewelry, their designer shoes. So she'd defiantly selected an outfit that showed off *her* assets.

Both of them were on the verge of yielding to temptation. "I've got to get out of here," she muttered.

"Claustrophobic?"

"Homicidal."

Pressing his hands to the tile wall, he leaned over her. "You know, it haunted me, that shower we never took together."

"What shower?" Anne asked breathlessly.

"That morning at your apartment." His distant gaze carried her back with him, to five years ago. "I was in such a hurry to get to work. I thought we'd have lots of time together, all those special moments. Afterward, I fantasized about how you would look with rivulets of water running down your body, and how your skin would smell."

"Now you have a chance to find out." Her throat was thick with longing.

"I do, don't I?" His cheek came down against hers and he sheltered her there, surrounding her, inhaling her. "How many more moments will we have, Anne?"

"Not many," she said regretfully. "We shouldn't even be having this one."

"I guess not." With a long release of breath, he moved away.

In the adjacent shower, the water started up. A minute later, a rushing noise filled the chamber on their other side as well.

That accounted for both of the new arrivals. If she didn't leave now, she'd have to wait an interminable time until both men were done changing.

"Want to risk it?" Eric asked. At her nod, he poked his head through the curtain and surveyed the room.

"All clear, although I can't see the outer room," he said.

If she gave herself time to worry, Anne knew she'd never move again. Instead, she thrust herself through the curtains and hurried out. Around the corner. Through the locker room, which was mercifully empty.

Thanking her stars, and wondering how she was going to get back to her room without arousing suspicions, Anne dripped her way along the hall. She entered the exercise room, her waterlogged tennis shoes squelching at every step.

Outside, she passed the swimming pool unnoticed. In the clear, finally!

Then she curved around the pro shop and nearly ran splat into Caroline.

Chapter Seven

The tall, perfectly coiffed bride-to-be stepped back with an expression of dismay. Impatiently, she flicked droplets of water off her fluffy pink sweater and charcoal-gray slacks.

"Good lord!" she said. "Aren't you a sight!"

"Sorry." Anne searched desperately for an explanation. "I had a little accident."

"You fell in the pool? Next time, try wearing a swimsuit," Caroline said. "You didn't happen to see Eric around, did you?"

"Eric?"

"You know, the groom?" Her carefully modulated voice dripped sarcasm. "I'm trying to find him."

"He, uh, went into the locker room."

"How did you happen to see that?" Caroline's eyes narrowed. "It opens off the gym, not the pool."

"I meant to say, he went into the gym." Anne could see she was digging herself in even deeper. She had to redirect the other woman's attention, quickly. "He made a rude comment about my being all wet. How can you marry such a boor?"

It occurred to her, too late, that she shouldn't have

insulted Caro's taste in men. The bride, however, merely smiled. "No one's perfect. A woman has to be prepared to change a man after they're married, anyway."

Anne knew she was venturing even further onto dangerous ground. She needed to know where Caroline stood, however. "You don't sound as if you love him."

"Love?" The other woman regarded her as if she'd said something ridiculous. "Of course I do. But men, well, sometimes it's hard to know what they feel."

"Eric does love you," she persisted. "Otherwise he wouldn't have asked you to marry him."

The response was a brittle laugh. "But he didn't. I simply announced that we were getting married and invited everyone to the engagement party. He wouldn't embarrass me in front of both our families."

"How could you do that?" Anne blurted.

Caroline's expression softened. "Because he owed it to me. All these years I've relied on him, confided in him, given him everything. He couldn't leave me!"

"Was he going to?" She could hardly breathe from the suspense.

"I—I don't know," the bride admitted. "It seemed like he was drifting away. I knew eventually he'd come back, like he always does, but I was tired of waiting. I just gave him a little nudge."

"I could never do anything like that," Anne said. "What if he called your bluff?"

"Oh, please!" Caroline sniffed. "Until you learn

to go after what you want, Anne, you'll never be anything but my mother's secretary.''

Without another word, the bride continued her stroll in the direction of the gym. Behind her, Anne stood stunned.

Eric hadn't proposed to Caroline. She'd manipulated him. Still, in the year since his engagement party, he hadn't called off the wedding. Why not?

The curious stares of two passing tennis players reminded her of her drenched condition. With a shiver, she set herself in motion.

She didn't fully understand why this revelation made her even angrier at Eric. Because he'd allowed himself to be manipulated? Or because he loved a woman who would do such a thing?

At the main hotel building, she skirted the brick terrace, where late risers were breakfasting, and entered by a side door. A service staircase took her to the third floor unobserved.

In her room, the staff had removed Eric's tray and made the bed. Through the door to Genevieve's sitting room, she heard the murmur of female voices. From the tones, it sounded like the kind of impersonal conversation that went on during a manicure or massage.

Thank goodness her boss wasn't expecting her back, because she was in no mood to make small talk. In the bathroom, Anne stripped off her soaking clothes and toweled dry. Catching a glimpse of herself in the mirror, she studied her reflection.

Straight brown hair in disarray, troubled green eyes, cheekbones too wide and a chin too pointed to be photogenic. She could never approach Caroline's chilly beauty.

Was that what Eric wanted? If so, why had he kissed her passionately in the locker room?

No doubt, as Caroline implied, Anne was too timid. Although she could be brave when it came to getting a story, she tended to retreat from personal conflicts.

Five years ago, when Laurie denied her a fair share of credit, Anne had gathered her tattered pride around her and left. It hadn't occurred to her until much later that she might have gained more by creating a scene at the office, and that a tongue-lashing might have made Laurie respect her in the end.

She'd also fled from her apartment rather than accuse Eric openly of deceit. What if she had faced him? At least she would have spared herself endlessly replaying an imaginary confrontation in the months that followed.

Finally, two years ago, after driving halfway across the country to interview at *The Loop,* she meekly accepted the news that the job was taken. If only she's raised a stink! Eric might have considered her for some other opening, even if it were merely copyediting.

Anne would never want to become as selfish as Caroline. That didn't mean she couldn't benefit from today's discovery, in her own way.

THE PROSPECT of seeing Anne at his cottage, even just long enough to get started on the article, lightened Eric's mood. When he ran into Caroline inside the workout room, he maintained his good cheer.

No, he couldn't go shopping in town with her for the rest of the morning, even though her bridesmaids had been inconsiderate enough to make themselves scarce. However, he promised to meet her for a late lunch at two o'clock. A peck on the cheek, a "You're looking lovely," and he was off, striding around the pond with an impulse to whistle.

Like a kid playing hooky.

Of course, he couldn't skip school forever. At two o'clock, the alarm would ring. Eric fully intended to make up to Caroline for his inattentiveness.

After ten years of dating her on and off, she'd become so familiar that he couldn't imagine life without her. He looked forward to the intimacies, the change in their relationship that marriage would bring. In the meantime, he wanted to throw a few more figurative spitballs and sail a few more paper airplanes behind the teacher's back.

"You certainly are in a good mood. But then, you probably slept well, which is more than I can say." The nasal voice of Montcrief DeLong jerked Eric out of his reverie.

He'd nearly reached the gazebo, en route to his cottage. Monty, his cheeks patched with a couple of bandages, stood on the path clutching a handful of spring flowers.

"Are those for me?" Eric joked.

"They're for Petsy Thorpe," said the younger man. "She's head of the fine arts charity ball next season, you know. I want to be sure she sends me tickets."

"She'll send them to the magazine." Eric wished his reporter would make himself scarce. The young man was blocking his route.

"I'd like my own set. I have to keep up my contacts, you know." As Monty brushed back his blond hair, it looked for a moment as if he were wearing a bouquet of flowers tucked over one ear. Not a pretty sight, Eric decided.

"I believe hotel policy discourages the guests from picking posies," he said. "You could purchase a bouquet at the flower shop."

"Don't talk to me about this hotel!" Monty glared at the flowers, then tossed them onto the water. A couple of swans glided over to investigate. "They've stuck me in a horrible room, and as for the bathroom, the lighting is impossible! I cut myself twice shaving."

Eric struggled to summon sympathy, and failed. "I hope the concierge provided free Band-Aids."

Monty sniffed. "The room stinks of the kitchen! And I hardly got any sleep, what with all the banging and thumping." He didn't elaborate, leaving Eric to try to imagine what might have made such noises. "I don't suppose you'd let me sleep on your couch, would you?"

"In Ivy Cottage?" Eric asked in disbelief. "No dice. By the way, how's the story coming?"

"Which, uh—? Oh, the wedding!"

"That is what you're supposed to be covering. What have you got?"

"Well, it hasn't happened yet, so what could I have?" grumbled the young man.

"Have you interviewed the chef about the food? Talked him out of a recipe?" Eric demanded. "How about the staff who are setting up tents, handling decorations, fixing hair? Statistics, details, color! Our readers want to smell the smells and taste the food."

"If I wanted smells, I could stay in my room!" sighed Monty. "Sorry! I'll see what I can find out." With a toss of his head, he strode away.

Eric reminded himself that he'd vowed to give the young man another chance to become a decent reporter. He hoped the kid would finally get his act together.

The young man's amusing style might yet save the day, if he buckled down and did a little research. Eric decided to reserve judgment until he saw the wedding story.

Besides, the further he got from the main building, now out of sight behind some trees, the more relaxed he felt. It was a relief to be away from Monty, from relatives, even from friends.

He approached the cottage slowly, hoping Anne was already there. Sure enough, he spotted her in profile, sitting on a flat stone bench beside a willow.

She wasn't exactly alone. The white cat for which he'd once mistaken her circled the bench, mewing as if trying to communicate.

Anne responded with a couple of credible "meows" of her own. After a bit of back-and-forth dialogue, the cat rolled onto its back and presented its tummy to be scratched.

"You little rascal." She rubbed the cat, which purred so loudly Eric could hear it from where he stood. "You just want a free massage."

"Can I get one, too?" he asked. The cat scrambled to its feet, shot him a reproachful look and prowled away.

"I'm afraid I have a strictly hands-off policy when it comes to you." Getting to her feet, Anne brushed off her tan blazer. Beneath it, she wore a striped jersey top over a beige skirt, Eric saw. Very business-like and yet, on her, intensely appealing. "We have a job to do."

"Then let's get started." He unlocked the cottage and stood aside. "How are my pheromones?"

Anne stepped inside. "Under control, I'd say."

"I chained them and threatened them with whips before I went out this morning."

"You should have done the same to yourself before you barged into my bedroom." She raised a hand to forestall his comeback. "Let's get down to work, shall we?"

On a day when the sun was shining and a person could go water-skiing on the lake? Or sit at an outdoor café? Or simply gaze into the face of a stubborn, elusive woman who made his pulse perform gold-medal gymnastics?

Dragging in a deep breath helped Eric get a grip on himself. Anne had taken a seat at the dining room table and was waiting for him to pull up the appropriate document on the laptop. He needed her help. If he didn't want to send her fleeing for cover, he'd better attend to business.

"I wish I'd brought a printer so we could run off a hard copy, but I wasn't expecting this." Deliberately averting his gaze from her, he switched on the computer. "I've jotted down the phone numbers for sources that one of my staff members provided." He indicated a sheet of Swan's Folly stationery.

After a few questions, Anne settled at the computer to read. Backlit by a window, strands of russet and wheat gleamed in her brown hair. The blandness of her clothing only emphasized the warmth of her coloring and the inviting contours of her figure.

Over the years, Eric had sometimes wished he had a photograph of Anne. Details of her appearance had blurred in his memory, until this weekend. Now he wondered how he could have forgotten her impish smile or the way that, even deep in concentration, her heart-shaped face never lost its air of sweetness.

For a time, she had been merely a warm memory. Now she was rapidly becoming more real than anyone else, even Caroline.

"By the way." Anne glanced up from the screen. "Petsy's husband saw a woman coming out of your cottage last night."

Eric blinked. "Caro didn't say anything. I just ran into her."

"I persuaded Genevieve that he saw me, and that I was standing by the window, not coming out the door," Anne said. "I hate lying. For some reason, I seem to be doing a lot of it these days."

"It *was* you that he saw," Eric pointed out.

"Oh. That part was true, I guess. I still feel as if I deceived my boss, and I don't like that."

He had kind of enjoyed this morning's games, especially the hiding-in-the-shower part, but he knew better than to say so. "What do you think of the story so far?"

She rested her chin on her palm. "This is interesting, about the Fantasy Dates service. I've never heard of people paying extra for a date in a costume before."

"Monty made it sound like a call-girl service," Eric said. "The owner strongly disagrees."

Anne jotted on a pad. "I'll talk to her. My impression is that either men or women can request a fantasy, or fulfill one, and that there's no guarantee of anything beyond companionship."

"It does look suspicious, though, since usually the men do the ordering," Eric noted. "And the women don't seem to mind accepting what's called a 'costume fee.'"

"So? How many of them have a harem outfit hanging in the back of their closet? Or—" Anne checked the screen "—bunny ears and a bow tie? They probably use the money to buy or rent their outfit."

Eric couldn't resist playing devil's advocate. "If a woman's seriously seeking love, why would she pose as something she's not?"

"Sometimes a woman needs to get out of a rut," Anne responded. "Maybe she wants to try on a new personality."

"By having a guy pay her to go drinking and dancing dressed like Madonna?"

"People don't always think rationally. Besides, a lady might want to shake off some of her inhibitions." Anne stood and stretched. Eric wondered if she had any idea how the movement called attention to her shapely breasts, or how it stirred his rebellious male urges. "To change the things that aren't working in her life. To make a guy see her as someone special."

"Even if it's false?"

"People play games all the time. I'll show you." Anne shrugged out of her jacket. Eric held himself rigidly in check.

Darting across the room, she swirled a silk shawl from the back of a love seat and wrapped it around the lower half of her face. Against the peacock-patterned cloth, her emerald eyes glinted and her skin gleamed like satin. The prosaic journalist became an alluring woman of the East.

Holding the scarf with one hand, Anne undulated

to unseen music. Eric could almost smell the incense. His hands flexed, and his hips began to sway to her rhythm. He could scarcely catch his breath.

"Well?" came her muffled voice.

He struggled to make a joke. "You forgot to say, 'Yes, master.'"

Anne lowered the scarf. "You see how a costume changes things?" She tossed it over the love seat and returned to her seat. "I think these ladies are trying on roles, not selling their bodies."

"So does the Fantasy Dates owner. The guys may have other ideas, though." *Just like me.*

"Guys usually do." Anne returned to her reading.

Eric tried to concentrate on the latest copy of a trade journal. He read the same story three times and still couldn't grasp what it was about.

His imagination remained lost in the Arabian nights. With Anne as Scheherazade, performing the dance of the seven veils.

At last, she let out a long breath that told him she'd finished going over the story. "Well?" he said.

"It's provocative. Funny in places, too," she said. "After what you've told me, though, it makes me uneasy. I hope I can get hold of this vice officer and make sure he wasn't quoted out of context."

Eric checked his watch. Although he'd be early for lunch with Caroline, he needed to get away from this cottage. From seductive images of Anne.

Besides, it wouldn't hurt to make himself visible at the hotel. He'd been neglecting his friends and relatives, and he felt an obligation to play match-maker between his brother and Bianca, both of whom were thickheaded as woolly mammoths.

"I'm sure you can handle it," he said. "I've got to meet my fiancée."

"I meant what I said. I'm not a ghostwriter." Anne closed the file and opened another one. To hold her notes, he presumed. "This is an editing job only."

"I know you won't let me down." Stifling a guilty pang at leaving her with what he was certain would be a major rewrite, Eric scooted out of the cabin.

He couldn't resist peeking back through the curtains. The light from the opposing window silhouetted her as she picked up his cell phone.

If he were going to order a fantasy date, Eric decided, he would unquestionably pick Anne in a veil. And as little else as possible.

AN HOUR LATER, Anne thanked the detective for his help and saved yet another screenful of notes.

She'd only talked to two sources so far, the police officer and the Fantasy Dates owner, and already she could see that Monty's story was more fiction than fact. Every person mentioned in the article would have to be contacted.

Eric must have realized this. He hadn't exactly denied it, she admitted silently. He hadn't hesitated to exploit her situation, either.

Gritting her teeth, Anne reminded herself that her presence here had freed him to spend the day with Caroline. Her duty, after all, was to ensure that this wedding took place as planned.

That didn't mean she had to like it, she reflected in annoyance as she dialed the next number on the list.

PINK AGAIN. Eric was beginning to feel claustrophobic.

Caroline wore a salmon-colored suit with rose embroidery around the jacket and matching frog-style closures in front. Their table on the hotel's rear terrace came with a spray of pink flowers tucked into a swan-shaped vase.

Beyond them lay the green sweep of lawn, the Folly, the rippling blue pond and the woods. He gulped in the fresh air and tried to concentrate on the ornate lunch menu.

"I'll have a scoop of low-fat cottage cheese," Caroline told the waiter who hovered at her elbow. "And some fruit—make sure it's fresh, not canned."

"We never serve canned fruit at Swan's Folly, Miss Knox," the man said.

"I want a bran muffin, no raisins. Fresh-squeezed orange juice without any sugar added, I don't care how tart it is. Decaf coffee with the meal. Please bring us some artificial sweetener, and I want a little pitcher of skim milk for my coffee."

"Yes, Miss Knox." The waiter finished scribbling. "Mr. Bellamy?"

"I'll have the grilled cheese and a root beer."

"Root beer?" said Caroline.

"With a side of pretzels," Eric added mischievously. "In honor of my father."

"What kind of cheese, sir?" said the waiter.

"Whatever you've got."

"Which kind of bread would you prefer?"

"It doesn't matter." He just wanted the man to go away. "Whole wheat would be fine." Mercifully, that did the trick; the waiter departed.

"If you don't ask for exactly what you want,

you'll never get it." With a wave of her hand, Caroline shooed a butterfly from their flowers.

"I did ask for exactly what I wanted." Eric searched for a neutral topic. "How was your morning?"

"Frustrating. Mother's playing grande dame in her suite and she's tied up the best hairdresser," Caroline said. "Oh, look, there's Petsy! Yoo-hoo!"

Eric half hoped his fiancée's irritating cousin would join them, at least long enough to give them something to talk about, until he noticed that she was towing her young son. Lambie, whose face seemed to be perpetually smeared with food, stuck out his tongue at a passing bellboy and blew a loud raspberry.

Clucking at him indulgently, Petsy waved back at Caro. "I promised Lambie he could go swimming with Fawn!" she called. "You know how he acts if he doesn't get his way!"

Kids were great, unless people spoiled them, Eric reflected. This little guy needed a strong hand, or he'd end up as self-absorbed as Monty DeLong. On the other hand, swimming wasn't a bad idea. At least he'd wash that food off his face.

"That kid could use some discipline," he said.

"What he needs is a nanny," Caroline said. "Petsy spends way too much time with him."

Petsy's devotion to her son, indulgent as it might be, was one of her better qualities, in Eric's view. "That's her job, so to speak."

"Being a leader of society is a job, too! So is staying beautiful!" Caroline extended her fingers, displaying long, petal-pink nails. "If there's one thing my mother's taught me, it's that a woman can't afford to let herself go. If she does, she won't have any friends left.''

"Real friends don't care what you look like.'' Reassuringly, Eric closed his hand over hers on the table.

Caroline stiffened, and he released her, troubled. Didn't she feel any need for physical contact?

During the early years of their courtship, she responded happily to his kisses and cuddling. However, she drew the line at anything more intimate and Eric respected her wish to save herself for her wedding night.

He'd assumed that she, too, had to fight her cravings for closeness. As the years went by, however, she'd cooled down until he wondered if she felt any physical desire at all.

Everyone, including their parents, assumed they were sleeping together. Caro had asked him not to make an issue of it, so he kept his mouth shut on the subject. That didn't mean that he could accept a passionless marriage.

There were a lot of topics they'd never discussed. The tone had been set a year ago, when Caroline shamefacedly admitted to Eric that she scheduled an engagement party.

Then she'd burst into tears. And apologized, and begged him not to shame her, and asked with trembling lips if she'd misunderstood him. Weren't they going to be married, sooner or later? Wasn't he her closest friend? Was she all alone in the world?

He hurried to reassure her. And, perhaps, himself, too. Well, Eric reflected grimly, he should have been tougher. At the very least, they should have discussed basic issues.

It was time to be honest with each other. To find out what was really on her mind, and make sure she understood what was on his.

With the sense of stepping onto quicksand, Eric leaned forward and said, ''Before it's too late, there are some matters we need to talk about. And we have to do it now.''

Chapter Eight

"Matters we need to talk about?" Caroline raised one eyebrow. "You're not going to spring a prenuptial agreement on me, are you?"

"Of course not." Eric believed that when people married, they joined their lives. He would happily share everything he had with his wife, even if she were as poor as Anne. "I mean personal matters."

Before he could elaborate, the waiter arrived with their food. Caroline proceeded to request margarine instead of butter, extra maraschino cherries with the cottage cheese, and a pitcher of ice water.

At last they were alone. Doggedly, Eric returned to his topic. "There are important areas we've never delved into."

"That's true!" Caro picked at the cloth napkin in her lap. "Like where we're going on our honeymoon."

He set down his grilled cheese sandwich. "That's not what I meant."

"You don't want to know?"

"I *was* meaning to ask you," he admitted. "Traditionally, it's the groom's job to arrange the honeymoon, isn't it? If you want me to take charge of it, I'd be happy to.''

He didn't suppose it would be difficult to book last-minute tickets to Hawaii. And for the heiress to a hotel chain, landing a suite was never a problem.

She nearly choked on her cottage cheese. ''After all the trouble I've gone to? We've got lovely rooms facing Central Park, and tickets to the latest Broadway hits. I've scheduled appointments with my favorite couturiers, and dinner at the best restaurants, and a party in the hotel ballroom for the most important people in the publishing industry!''

''During our honeymoon?'' He wondered if he'd misunderstood her. Honeymoons meant lazy days at the beach or in a mountain cabin or by a pool. ''We need time to get to know each other.''

''We've known each other for years!''

''Not in the Biblical sense.''

Caroline poured two packets of sweetener in her coffee and added three precise drops of skim milk. ''You hardly ever take a break from working, so I didn't want to waste our time.''

''You consider throwing a party for the publishing industry an appropriate activity for a honeymoon?''

''You need to make more contacts,'' she said. ''Otherwise, how are you ever going to move up?''

''Move up?'' Eric repeated. ''I do plan to start a second magazine, once I settle on the concept. Right now, though, I've got some staffing problems to contend with.''

She cut the bran muffin into bite-size pieces. ''Surely you don't plan to stay in Chicago forever. New York is the center of the publishing world.''

''Chicago is my niche.'' Eric wondered where

these ambitions had sprung from. Caroline had certainly never mentioned them before. "I know this area and I care about it. I can also see where the best publishing opportunities lie."

"Last night, you said you wanted me to take more interest in your work," she flared. "Well, I'm tired of sitting on the sidelines, and you should be too!"

"You've changed," he said.

"As my mother keeps pointing out, I'm going to be thirty in a couple of years," Caro said. "It's time I set some goals for myself."

"Such as?" he probed.

"By next year, I want to be living in New York." For the first time in months, Caro's face shone with enthusiasm. "We're going to be on everyone's A-list for parties. When we go to the opera, the paparazzi will be all over us. Maybe I'll start my own show on cable...my family can sponsor it. Who knows more about style and beauty than I do?"

Eric's usually quick mind was having a hard time absorbing this burst of information. Caro wanted a career on television? She expected him to move to New York?

"I can't publish a magazine called *The Loop* from Manhattan," he said. "Besides, what about children?"

"What about them?"

"You do want them, don't you? Not right away, but in a year or so?"

"You've never mentioned children before." In her distress, Caroline swallowed a piece of muffin unchewed. He could see the lump going down her slender throat, but she managed to down the morsel with only a ghost of a cough.

"I'm not asking you to be a hausfrau with curlers in your hair," he said. "But children are very important to me."

"Oh, well, I suppose so. One or two." Quickly, she added, "I'd like to have them before I'm thirty-five, but I do need to establish myself in New York first."

He wished he didn't feel as if he were negotiating a business deal. "I haven't agreed to move anywhere."

"You'll love it!" Caroline beamed. "You know I go twice a year for shopping trips."

"And once to Paris," he pointed out.

"Yes. Anyway, I'm sure this honeymoon will change your mind. You'll absolutely go wild over the people, the excitement, the stimulation!"

"A man has a different kind of stimulation in mind on his honeymoon." Eric hadn't forgotten about his concern on that score.

"Don't be crass," said his wife-to-be. "Promise we can at least take an apartment in New York! After all, if we don't hurry, how will I find time to produce children before I'm thirty-five?"

"I can't give you an instant answer." He needed time to absorb this 180-degree twist in his life plan. "Caroline, you can't make one-sided decisions like this. There are two of us now."

"Somebody has to plan for the future!" She crumpled her napkin tightly.

Where had she gone, the vulnerable woman who'd poured out her heart to him? The girl who looked up to Eric and depended on him? Obviously, she'd changed more than he realized.

Am I making the biggest mistake of my life by marrying this woman?

Before that thought had a chance to settle, he spotted his future father-in-law crossing the terrace toward them. Under the circumstances, the interruption was welcome.

"Excuse me, kids." Hainsworth Knox gave his daughter a brief smile. "Eric, we're having some problems with the media. I thought perhaps you could help us."

"Of course." He couldn't leave on such an unsettled note, however. "Caro, you're right, I did invite this discussion. I'm glad you brought things out in the open."

"You'll consider my request?"

"Certainly."

Setting aside his napkin, he followed the hotel executive through the lobby and onto the front steps. Before him, the usually placid scene, with its meandering driveway and discreetly landscaped parking area, had taken on the air of a fortress under siege.

Beyond the wrought-iron main gate and front fence thronged an army of the press. A small army, Eric amended. He counted three camera crews, half a dozen photographers and roughly a dozen more reporters.

At the sight of him, a clamor went up. "Over here, Mr. Bellamy!"

"So where are you spending the night *before* the wedding, Eric?"

"Is it true Caroline's changed her mind about the dress three times?"

The irony was that he actually knew some of these people from his earlier years as a journalist. That didn't mean they would cut him any slack, now that he'd become the topic du jour.

And what a topic he would be, if he called off the wedding now! How could he bring that kind of public humiliation on Caro, on kind, patient Hainsworth, or on the rest of their friends and family? If he and his bride had differences, they would have to resolve them.

Stepping forward, Eric raised his hands for silence. "Whoa! If you guys want a press conference, I'll give you one."

Minicams began rolling. "Are you going to make a video available of the wedding?" an announcer demanded. "We need clips immediately after the ceremony!"

"No videotape." The Knoxes and the Bellamys had both agreed that, no matter what the modern trend in recording weddings might be, color photographs were good enough for them. "This is a private affair."

"Where are you spending tonight?" called a woman.

"At my bachelor party," Eric said. "With my male friends and relatives."

He declined to mention that it would be held on a yacht on Lake Geneva. If these vultures got wind of where he was going, he'd have no privacy at all. As it was, he'd have to sneak off the premises in the back of a limousine.

"Having any second thoughts?" shouted someone else.

"Don't be ridiculous!" The response came automatically, thank goodness. Eric knew that any hesitation on his part would have been seized upon and dissected at length.

"What kind of food is being served at the wedding dinner?" asked a woman he recognized as a life-styles writer for a Chicago-area newspaper.

"This is Mr. Hainsworth Knox, CEO of the Lambert hotel chain. He's also my future father-in-law," Eric said. "I'm going to let him tell you about the menu."

Although an unassuming man in private life, Hainsworth rose to the occasion. "We've brought in two of our finest chefs from our other hotels to assist the excellent Swan's Folly chef," he said. "Crates of lobsters are being flown in early tomorrow morning."

Grateful for these social register tidbits, the press focused on him. Eric seized the chance to slip away.

As he headed for his cottage, he felt as if he'd narrowly escaped from danger. Not at the hands of the press, but from his own uncertainties.

Of course, he couldn't abandon Caroline virtually at the altar. The honeymoon plans weren't really such a big deal. And lots of wealthy people maintained a residence in New York as well as in their home community.

It was a relief to put his doubts aside. Eric never let people down. He didn't intend to start now.

ANNE RUBBED the back of her neck where it ached from bending over the computer. She'd spent all afternoon interviewing people and was only partway through her revisions. Although she preserved a few funny lines and the general structure of Monty's story, little else survived.

For this she would receive a tiny credit at the end saying that she contributed to the story?

She tried telling herself that reporting was more interesting than doing secretarial work, which was what Genevieve had sent her for. And that she'd done her duty by freeing Eric to spend the afternoon with his bride. It didn't ease the dissatisfaction.

"Until you learn to go after what you want, Anne, you'll never be anything but my mother's secretary."

A key scraped in the lock. Eric entered, whistling.

The air of the room altered as he came in. He radiated a subtle electrical current that made it thrum on his own personal frequency.

The man had a confident, almost cocky air, as if he'd polished off a few foes without breaking a sweat. With a lurch of pain, Anne wondered if he and Caroline had found time to be alone in the bridal suite.

She didn't want to picture the two of them together. To imagine how glorious it would feel to be Eric's bride, to lift that silky blue-green shirt off his torso and trace her tongue lightly along his chest...

She forced a lightness into her voice. "You must have had a good time at lunch."

He shot her a startled look. "Oh, hi, Anne. I forgot you were here."

"That's flattering."

A grin curved upward, slightly higher on one side, giving him a rakish air. With his dark hair and his athletic build, Eric exuded masculine appeal. "No offense intended. How's it going?"

"Slowly." With an effort, she gathered her wits. "This isn't just an editing job. Monty's going to need a magnifying glass to find what's left of his story."

"I'll make him sit down and compare them side by side. Maybe he'll learn something." Eric sauntered toward the stairs.

"Don't you want to see it?"

"I'll read it later," he said. "I need a jog to work off my meal."

He needed a jog? That didn't sound like a man who'd just made love to his fiancée. Although she knew it was foolish, Anne felt a spurt of relief.

"We have to talk about my byline." Darn, it felt awkward, confronting him when he was in such a cheerful mood. "I think I deserve equal credit with the original writer."

"A joint byline?" he said on his way up. "Do you really believe that's appropriate?"

She bit back a retort, that she'd deserved a shared byline five years ago and she deserved one now. What was the use of dragging out their old quarrel?

He vanished into his bedroom. Anne returned to pounding the keyboard.

She wondered why he and Caroline *weren't* spending more time in the bedroom. Or any time, as far as she could tell.

Maybe the bride was deliberately keeping her groom hungry. To Anne, that hardly seemed like a tactic to guarantee fidelity.

At last Eric reappeared in running shorts and a T-shirt, with a towel draped over one shoulder. To wipe away any sweat that threatened his chiseled perfection, no doubt.

"Well?" she said. "Are we going to discuss my byline now?"

"I'll take it under consideration." With a wave, he went out the door.

Anne barely restrained the urge to seize the laptop and hurl it after him.

BY THE TIME Eric finished his jog, his good mood was beginning to fray. For one thing, he'd run into his brother and discovered that Neill still hadn't figured out the obvious, that he was the father of Bianca's baby and that she needed him. How dense could a guy be? And why had he himself ever promised to keep his stepsister's secret?

For another thing, he wished he had a better answer to Anne's request. She was right; she deserved a byline. But to take away half the credit from a regular staffer and give it to a freelancer would be a slap in Monty's face.

As for the change in Caroline, he was glad to see her gaining in self-confidence. She'd gone a bit overboard in her plans, but...

Then he saw her, sitting on the bench near his cottage where Anne had waited earlier. Approaching quietly in his jogging shoes, he had a chance to observe his fiancée in a rare moment of contemplation. In profile, her features resembled the perfection of a high-fashion model.

"Oh, there you are!" Standing up, Caroline picked a speck of dust from her pink suit. "Mummy's secretary said you'd be back soon, but I didn't care to wait inside."

"You talked to Anne?" he asked.

"It was nice of Mummy to lend her to you." She might have been talking about a piece of equipment. "I've had the most wonderful idea! I couldn't wait to discuss it."

The prospect of dealing with another of Caro's

bright ideas was daunting. As she herself had pointed out, though, it was Eric who'd suggested they share more. "Fire away."

"You *do* want me to understand your business, don't you?" She moved out of a ray of sunlight; Caroline was always careful not to overexpose her skin. "And don't forget, in New York we'll be throwing a party for all those publishing honchos. How tedious for me to be introduced as your wife, period. People will think I'm just a tagalong who doesn't know anything."

"What did you have in mind?" he asked.

She smoothed down her skirt. "I want you to make me some kind of editor on *The Loop*. Contributing editor, how does that sound? I could contribute gossip and style tips. Maybe write my own column! You can get me a ghostwriter, like everyone has these days."

Eric stared at her. The woman's capacity for taking him aback must be setting some kind of record.

He knew he should speak diplomatically, even promise to consider her suggestion. He might have done that if he hadn't been so aware of Anne laboring nearby for little credit and less money, and of how much she'd lost because despite talent, hard work and experience, she lacked connections.

Besides, it wasn't fair to Caroline to humor her like a child. A grown woman deserved an honest answer.

"I know that a lot of people succeed on nothing more than hype and having the right contacts," he said. "However, I'm old-fashioned enough to believe that accomplishments ought to be earned."

Caro's jaw dropped. Her blue eyes fixed on him in disbelief.

"You might try writing a column on your own," he continued, struggling to be fair. "Maybe you'll turn out to have a knack for it and, if so, I'd love to hire you. But I can't hand you a plum position when a number of freelance writers would kill for a job at *The Loop.* Writers who've done a good job for me and who know their craft." He intentionally made the reference general; no sense in letting her know he had anyone specific in mind.

His fiancée caught her breath. "Really? And are you planning to marry any of those freelance writers?"

"Certainly not."

"Then I shouldn't have to compete with them!" She stamped her foot so hard she cracked a twig. "Eric Bellamy, how can you be like this?"

With tears of anger glittering in her eyes, she strode away. He suspected she was waiting for him to call out an apology. If so, she was going to be disappointed.

In frustration, Eric thumped his forehead against a tree. Why had he ever brought up the possibility of involving Caroline with his work? Yet that publishing party idea of hers must have been in the works for weeks.

Leaves rustled, coming toward him. "Are you all right?" It was Anne's voice, low and concerned.

"Did you know Caroline had invited New York's publishing elite to a party?" He kept his face to the tree.

"Of course. Who do you think sent all the invitations?" she asked.

"Why didn't you tell me?"

"She said it was a surprise."

"It certainly is." He wanted to punch someone. Not Anne, though. "How's the article?"

"It's finished. Probably a few rough edges, but I assume you'll read it over."

"Tomorrow." He couldn't concentrate this afternoon. On anything.

He felt her gaze burning the back of his neck. "I don't suppose there's any use bringing up the question of my byline again."

Vaguely, Eric recalled reading a fairy tale in which a tree wrapped itself around someone and engulfed him. He wished that might happen for real. It would be a lot easier than dealing with the people and emotions pulling and pushing at him. "Sorry."

"Don't stand there too long," said Anne. "The cat might come by and mark you."

He heard her moving off. This time, he wished he could call out an apology and summon her back. But he didn't.

Chapter Nine

The sweep and the scope of the ballroom at Swan's Folly brought to mind photos Anne had seen of the palace at Versailles. From overhead, crystal chandeliers cast dimples of light across a sea of white-draped tables. On the far side, an array of glass doors opened onto a broad verandah.

The small contingent of ladies invited to the bachelorette party clustered in the middle of the room like travelers shipwrecked on a desert island. The decorous music provided by a male harpist and a string ensemble did nothing to rescue the occasion.

Neither Genevieve, imperious in a lace gown with bell-shaped sleeves, nor Caroline, wearing a flowered crepe georgette dress and pearls, seemed to mind. They nodded approvingly at the pink and white balloons floating from the tables and decorously sampled the sugary marzipan flowers, overly sweet cake and the punch, which to Anne tasted as if it had been spiked with cheap liquor.

The only lively note came from Nana Lambert, aflutter in lavendar chiffon. She went around whispering to people that she planned to perform a dance in the bride's honor.

"I certainly hope she doesn't carry out her threat," Genevieve said to Anne. "Really, Caro's already upset about something or other. I just want everything to be perfect for my daughter." She dabbed her lipstick with a napkin on which was printed "June 18— Caroline's Last Night as Miss Knox."

Judging by Eric's distracted mood a couple of hours ago, Anne suspected the bride had bigger problems than whether her party came off without a hitch. However, for her employer's sake, she hoped things proceeded smoothly.

Into the room swished Petsy Lambert, wearing an Edwardian flowered top with leg-of-mutton sleeves over a dark-green skirt. "Goodness, everyone's been raiding Elizabeth Muldoon's samples from The Velvet Fig!" sniffed Genevieve. "I hope she hasn't depleted the stock. I have an investment in that store."

"She gave me this, too, you know!" Winnie burbled as she slipped into a seat beside Anne. "See, Daddy told me to wear something old-fashioned, so I did!"

With a giggle, she spread her arms to display her outfit. Although the flowered skirt reached nearly to her ankles, the skimpy red velvet vest was obviously designed to be worn over a blouse. The bride's little sister, however, had chosen to maximize her exposure. In fact, if she wiggled much harder, her private assets might become a public offering.

"Winnifred! Go and change!" said Genevieve.

"Mummy!"

"Now!"

From her purse, the young woman pulled a fringed shawl. "How's this?" With a rebellious flounce, she wrapped it around herself.

Further down the table, Caroline glared at her sister. "How ugly! You look like the little old lady who lived in a shoe."

"That reminds me!" Winnie plopped her feet onto the white linen tablecloth. "Anne, did you see my new shoes? Aren't they fantastic?"

From their pointy black suede toes to the intricate assembly of laces twining around Winnie's ankles, the shoes were indeed fantastic. Anne, who never paid much attention to her shoes as long as they didn't hurt, became keenly aware that her own plain pumps were worn. Thank goodness they were hidden by the tablecloth.

"Winnie! Put your feet down!" demanded the mother of the bride.

"Oh, pooh!" Down they went with a thump. One of them plopped onto Anne's left foot. "I'm sorry!"

"It's all right," she said automatically. Then she glanced at her beige pump and saw that it had suffered a major black scuffmark across the top.

She couldn't help stealing a glance at Caroline's feet. The bride wore dressy sandals; the pink straps were connected by seashell-shaped gauze insets embroidered with faux pearls.

Anne resolved to toss her old shoes in the trash and replace them. There was nothing she could do about it tonight, though.

Across the room, Nana approached a pile of audio equipment and tried to insert a music tape for her dance. "How strange," she said. "There's already a tape in here. I wonder whose it is."

"Would somebody please stop her?" Genevieve grumbled.

When her boss said "somebody," she meant her

assistant. Reluctantly, Anne stood and started toward Nana.

"Mrs. Lambert?" she asked when she was half-way there. In the huge space, her words dwindled and vanished.

A loud knock on the ballroom's interior doors startled her and most of the other party goers. "Goodness!" Nana smoothed her billowing dress. "It must be one of my admirers."

A couple of busboys entered, wheeling an enormous wedding cake decorated with tissue-paper roses and, in sparkly letters, the names *Caroline* and *Eric*. Clapping her hands together in approval, Nana executed an impromptu jig.

"There must be some mistake!" Genevieve's stentorian voice silenced the string ensemble. "We didn't order this."

At that moment, the stereo equipment sprang into action, apparently triggered by remote control, although Anne couldn't tell who had done the deed. From the speakers blared a raucous piece of music.

Off the cardboard cake popped the glittery top. Genevieve and Caroline uttered identical gasps of horror as out leaped a muscular young man, his entire body painted gold.

The only clothing he wore, as far as Anne could see, were a gold lamé loincloth, a stiff white collar, a black-and-white polka-dot tie and white cuffs. To the dismay of the ladies, with the possible exceptions of Winnie and Nana, he began undulating and fiddling with his tie.

Now Anne remembered the name of the tune. It was "The Stripper."

THE LOOP had once run an article on bachelor parties as the last primitive male ritual remaining in an overly domesticated society. For the life of him, Eric couldn't remember what else the article had said, probably because he'd just guzzled more Scotch in one evening than he usually drank in a month.

In his fuzzy brain, Caroline had become the broom in the Disney version of "The Sorcerer's Apprentice." Every time he tried to chop one of her projects down to size, two more sprang up and threw buckets of water at him.

If only Anne were here. Anne always knew what to do. But he was far away from her, stuck on a boat and rapidly becoming too plastered to move.

Although he was glad to escape the hotel and its besieging horde of reporters, Eric would not have chosen to confine himself to a yacht sailing around Lake Geneva. Below decks at the bar, he was beginning to feel both claustrophobic and seasick. To make matters worse, the air in the *Truelove* was choked with cigar smoke from men playing poker and watching a heavyweight fight on cable TV.

Eric didn't even know most of them. His father had planned this party, and as far as he could see, most of the guests were aging pals of Budge's.

Shakily, he made his way up a staircase to the deck. Mercifully, the fresh air cleared his head enough for him to appreciate the magical quality of the lights twinkling from mansions along the banks.

Near the bow, Eric leaned on the brass railing. As his thoughts came into focus, he discovered that he was angry, but he wasn't sure at whom. At Caroline, for finally starting to grow up? Or at himself, for not having seen the changes earlier?

He turned at the sound of approaching footsteps. It was his older brother, Neill. They'd been close once, but they'd followed different paths as adults.

One of Eric's greatest regrets was that the two of them rarely saw each other. The man marched to his own drummer, and always had.

When, as a self-conscious teenager, Eric had undergone cosmetic surgery to correct a hereditary foot deformity that affected most of the Bellamys, Neill had refused. In fact, he'd defiantly gone barefoot at the country club whenever he got the chance, glaring down anyone who stared.

Budge's many marriages had left Neill with a hearty mistrust of the wedded state. Although he agreed to serve as best man, he made no secret of his doubts that any marriage could endure. Eric was beginning to wish he'd listened.

They stood in silence for a few minutes, staring at the dappled reflections of the yacht's lights on the lake. "Just think," Eric muttered, "tomorrow at this time I'll be married."

Or tell me it's going to be all right. It surprised him how much he yearned for his big brother's support.

Neill didn't notice. "Quit giving me the runaround about Bianca," he said. "I want the truth!"

"I can't break a confidence," Eric said. "Why don't you talk to her yourself?"

"I have. It didn't do any good." Downstairs, male voices cheered a blow by one of the prizefighters. Neill rambled on, his words blurring in Eric's befuddled mind, until he heard, "If you're the father of that baby, I have a right to know!"

Eric wondered if the alcohol might be causing hallucinations. He couldn't have heard his brother correctly. "You think *I'm* the father?"

"I knew you'd deny it!"

Had the man gone raving mad? "Of course I deny it." But Neill went on lambasting him.

It was useless trying to follow a conversation that made no sense. How dare his brother be so thickheaded just when Eric needed him most?

He grabbed Neill by his lapels. "Get this through your thick skull once and for all. I'm *not* the father!" he roared.

The next thing he knew, someone's fist flew through the air. He might have attributed it to one of the deckhands, except that it was attached to his own arm.

Neill ducked. Out of nowhere materialized two of their stepbrothers, Joe and Kevin. "Take it easy, guys," said Kevin, the younger of the pair.

"Have the captain stop at the next dock," Neill ordered Eric. "I'm getting off."

Since he had no idea who the captain was or whether he could pull over before they completed their circuit of the lake, Eric blustered, "The captain takes his orders from me and he's not stopping!"

Neill glowered. Then he vaulted over the rail and dived into the water.

"How much did he have to drink?" asked Joe. "The man could go into shock." Without waiting for an answer, Joe—a fireman—stripped off his jacket and jumped after Neill.

Below in the water, Eric made out the shape of his brother, swimming toward the nearest dock, and another dark form following at a distance. "Anyone else want a swim?'' he asked. ''How about me? I could use the exercise.''

''You're so far gone, you'd drown and not even know it.'' Kevin hauled him away from the railing. ''I would like to get this boat to stop, though. I want to go see what's happening at the bachelorette party.''

''Anne. Anne is happening,'' he sighed.

''Yeah, she's really interesting,'' Kevin said. ''That woman's too smart to be Genevieve's whipping girl. But what I meant was, one of the girls and I played this little joke. You know, a male stripper jumping out of a cake. Boy, I wish I could be there to see Caroline's face! She's such a stiff-necked—''

He halted in midsentence as it dawned on the young man, finally, to whom he was speaking. His jaw worked and some burbling noises came out.

Eric remembered the freelance swinging fist and wondered where it had gone. It seemed to him that it might be usefully employed in this situation.

Mostly, however, he was concerned about the news that a naked man would be making an appearance in Anne's vicinity. A well-built naked man, no doubt. ''So this guy,'' he said, ''this stripper. Is he looking for a girlfriend?''

''I think he's engaged to somebody,'' said Kevin. ''If it's okay with you, I'm going to find the captain so we can get off the boat. Okay?''

''Absolutely.''

CHAOS ERUPTED as the stripper gyrated atop a table. To make matters worse, he leaned down and set his stiff white collar atop Caroline's hair.

''Mummy!'' wailed the bride. ''Do something!''

"Leave it to me!" cried Nana, as she grabbed the gold-painted hunk. "Orchestra! A tango!" She proceeded to partner the man in an R-rated series of bumps and grinds, accompanied by the confused harpist.

"Who would do this to me?" cried Caroline.

"I know who," Genevieve snarled. "It's that woman who wants to get her hooks into Eric. She's so jealous she's trying to spoil everything!"

"Which woman?" Personally, Anne suspected Winnie of staging the prank, although the younger Knox girl was doing her best to keep a straight face. She wouldn't be surprised if Winnie had spiked the punch, too.

As for Eric's supposed pursuers, one of the usual suspects, dark-haired Lizzie, was staring in openmouthed horror at the goings-on. If she were suppressing glee, this had to be an Academy Award performance.

Genevieve ignored Lizzie. Instead, she stalked toward a pretty blond woman, Bianca, who must have left her baby with a sitter for the evening. "You— you—!" sputtered the bride's mother.

Bianca's eyes widened like a frightened doe's. Anne was trying to figure out how to intervene gracefully when through the doors stomped Neill Bellamy, dark and dripping like a creature dredged from the sea.

He drew himself up, towering over Genevieve. They fixed each other with cold stares. Then Neill shook himself like a wet dog, and Genevieve stepped back, gasping.

Seizing Bianca's arm, Eric's brother steered her

out into the night. "Good riddance!" snapped Genevieve, furiously brushing droplets from her dress.

She doused her fury with a glass of punch. "You know, this stuff isn't bad," she said, and dipped another glassful.

When the ersatz tango chugged to an end, Nana began organizing the guests into a conga line. Vivian, who had scarcely batted an eye at her elder son's disheveled appearance, waved to Genevieve. "Come join us!"

"I couldn't!"

"Why not?" asked Anne. "The steps aren't difficult."

"It isn't that. In fact, I used to be quite a dancer in my day," her boss told Anne. "Took voice lessons, too. I had this silly idea about going on the stage. Can you imagine?"

"You should join them," Anne said. "You'd have fun for a change. Besides, you've got such lovely shoes. Why not kick them up?"

"Don't be ridiculous." It was Caroline, returning from the corner where she'd withdrawn with her cell phone. "Listen, Mummy, I can't reach Eric. His phone is out of service and when I called the yacht, Daddy said he got off."

"He got off?" her mother repeated. "In the middle of the lake? Whatever for?"

"I don't know!" Caroline cried. "Maybe he's meeting someone. The way he's been acting, I wouldn't put it past him!"

Genevieve peered around the room. "Bianca's with Neill, but where did Elizabeth go? Has anyone seen her?"

"She *was* here." Anne wished her boss would

stop acting so paranoid. "He probably took a limo home so he could get some sleep. Tomorrow's a big day."

"Daddy said Eric drank too much and insisted on getting off at some dock in the middle of nowhere," Caroline protested. "He *had* to be meeting someone. He certainly couldn't take a limo!"

"If he drank too much, he might be trying to walk home," Anne pointed out.

"Oh, dear." Genevieve glanced enviously at the other ladies, who were giggling and cheering as they snaked around the ballroom. "We can't have him getting lost, or hit by a car. Can you imagine if he didn't show up for the ceremony tomorrow and we had to do the whole thing over? I don't think I can bear another weekend like this one."

"I'll look for him!" Caro declared. "Even though I'm so mad I almost wish he'd fallen in the lake like his brother. Do you know what Eric did, Mummy? He refused to make me a contributing editor at *The Loop* unless I actually write my own column! As if my inside knowledge weren't worth ten crummy ghostwriters!"

The blood drained from Anne's cheeks. All Caroline had to do was scribble a column, and Eric would hire her?

Amid cheers, the conga line ended. Nana and Vivian signaled madly to Genevieve. "Come here! In the name of love!" Nana demanded.

Genevieve regarded her mother with mingled exasperation and amusement before addressing her daughter. "You can't go driving around at night, dear. It isn't safe."

"Then make Anne go!" Caroline snapped. "I

won't have him showing up bandaged like King Tut because he had an accident! I want my wedding photos to be perfect!''

Genevieve frowned as if she were seeing her daughter in a not particularly flattering light. ''If it's dangerous for you to go out, it would be dangerous for Anne, too. However, she does have a more level head on her shoulders.''

''Do hurry, darling!'' called Nana. ''We need you!''

Despite the size of the ballroom, the walls were closing in on Anne. She didn't think she could bear one more minute in Caroline's presence and, despite her anger at Eric, she didn't want to see him come to harm, either.

''I don't mind taking a drive,'' she said. ''I'll cruise around the lake and see if I can spot him.''

''Thank you, dear.'' Genevieve patted her hand. ''You are my pillar, you know.''

Your husband should be your pillar, Anne thought, *and he would be, if you'd give him half a chance.* One of these days, she was going to say so.

''Don't stand there! Get moving!'' Caroline might have been addressing either her mother or her mother's assistant. Both of them instinctively backed away from her.

The last thing Anne noticed as she departed was her employer lining up with the groom's mother and Nana. To the flustered accompaniment of the harpist, they began belting out an off-key rendition of the Supremes song, ''Stop! In the Name of Love.''

Genevieve linked arms with the other women and kicked like a chorus girl. The sound of her laughter accompanied Anne out of the ballroom.

Chapter Ten

She left the windows down in her ten-year-old car as she cruised through the balmy evening. A light breeze brought the scents of night-blooming flowers and of bratwurst cooking at a German restaurant.

During her two years in Chicago, Anne had accompanied Genevieve to Lake Geneva on several occasions and had come to love its atmosphere of casual elegance. Located only a day's ride from the metropolis, it had been a popular getaway spot for more than a century.

Summer homes, country inns, hotels and condos sprawled along the shores of the lake. The expanses of flowers, the orchards and the old-fashioned architecture filled Anne with a sense of nostalgia.

Her headlights glimmered along the narrow road, which wound between vine-draped stone fences. On a Friday night, she wasn't surprised to hear distant music, but she saw no one moving around.

In this dark, woody setting, a man might easily get lost. With the weather so mild, she doubted Eric would come to any harm if he slept off his binge under a tree. However, tomorrow *was* his wedding day.

The fascinating man who'd claimed her heart five years ago and never relinquished it was going to walk down the aisle with Caroline in less than twenty-four hours. Anne knew she had to accept that reality, even though a part of her refused to.

She understood his desire to choose a woman of his own social class and economic status. Yet why were there no signs of affection between him and his bride? Not to mention the fact that Caroline had admitted manipulating him into the engagement.

On the verge of sympathizing with Eric, Anne reminded herself that he'd offered his wife-to-be a coveted position as a columnist for his magazine simply because she wanted it. All Caro had to do was jot down the words and leave them for someone else to rewrite.

Eric hadn't learned a thing from his mistake in hiring Monty DeLong, had he? Or maybe he didn't care how many real writers he exploited as long as his magazine carried bylines with snob value.

Anne's jaw tightened. Much as she cared about Genevieve, she would be glad when she could resign and never have to see these people again.

Ahead, the road curved past a small knot of shops, dark-timbered in the German style. Noticing some bright lights, she wondered in surprise if the stores could still be open. Her dashboard clock had died long ago, but the hour must be close to ten.

As she got closer, she saw that only one sign was lit. Old-style lettering proclaimed the name, Milady's Slippers.

Anne pictured the nasty scuff on her shoe. Darn it, she was tired of feeling like somebody's poor relation, and she knew she wouldn't have another chance to shop this weekend.

Impulsively pulling into a parking space, she stared at the large window. Against a green felt background, an assortment of elegant shoes competed for her attention.

The heels that drew her eye were velvet, wine-colored with a flat black bow on top. Subtle and proud. Anne could picture herself dancing in them until dawn, in the arms of a man with a smoldering gaze. A man who would sweep her off her feet and carry her home.

Milady's slippers, indeed. If the shoes fit, she would wear them.

When she reached the door, however, she found it locked. Inside, an older woman rearranging boxes didn't notice the tapping at first. When she did, she turned and mouthed the word, *Closed.*

Lifting her foot, Anne pointed to the ruined shoe. Then she interlaced her fingers in a mock prayer and mouthed back, "Please?"

The woman set down a box and came to the door. She stared at Anne's shoe. "Oh, dear, we can't have that," she said, and unlocked it.

They had only one pair of the wine-colored shoes left. Mercifully, it proved to be Anne's size. She didn't care that the price was triple what she usually paid.

She floated to her car in the lovely slippers, cushioned on air. In her imagination, stars glittered at her earlobes and against her bare throat.

Into the back seat she tossed the old pumps as she seized the reins, aka the steering wheel. Tonight, Anne was a princess driving her own coach. She knew she would find her prince, even if he did turn out to be drunk as a skunk.

Half a mile further, she saw the silhouette of a man sitting on a stone wall with his back to her. He faced the lake, his stillness a contrast to the shimmering water visible beyond a low-lying house.

Anne knew those strong shoulders. What she couldn't figure out was why Eric would choose to sit here alone on the eve of his wedding.

When she got out of the car, the slamming noise made him twitch. He settled down without further reaction.

"Eric!" she called. "I came to take you home."

He swung halfway around and sat profiled against the rippling lake. The classic symmetry of his straight nose and strong chin vanished, however, when he sneezed. "Sorry," he said. "I couldn't find my limo."

"You must have gotten off at the wrong dock."

He patted the wall beside him. "Sit."

It looked cold, and she didn't want to risk damaging her shoes. None of that mattered. Tonight was Eric's swan song as the unmarried Mr. Bellamy. She could still be his friend and sit by him, one last time.

The slope of the land and an accumulation of fallen stones eased her climb. A moment later, Anne scooted into place beside Eric on the wall.

Their feet dangled above a rosebush, its blooms silver in the moonlight. Further down the slope, a house lay sleeping, while beyond it, on the lake, lights outlined several yachts. The encircling shoreline twinkled as if it had been invaded by fairies.

Upward from the rosebushes wafted a fresh scent, sweet and almost unbearably innocent. That was the quality perfumes never captured, Anne thought, the innocence of uncut flowers.

"You're here." Eric's low voice blended with the night breeze. "Thank you."

"We heard you'd left the boat. Why did you?" The calm of their surroundings drained Anne's voice of any rebuke.

"I was worried about you," he said.

"About me?"

"The naked man." She caught a whiff of Scotch on his breath, which made her suspect he was babbling nonsense. "The one in the cake."

"Oh! The stripper," she said. "What about him?"

"He was near you." Eric measured his speech carefully, slurring only a little.

"And a couple of dozen other women," she pointed out.

"I don't like naked men near you," he said.

The remark startled a laugh from Anne. It vanished amid the churring of nightbirds and the distant hum of air-conditioning units.

"What's so funny?" he said.

"You don't like naked men near me?" Anne said. "What's that supposed to mean?"

"Unless it's me." Eric rested his arm around her back. "Not here, of course."

"Not anywhere," said Anne.

"I'm forgetting something, aren't I?" He ran his free hand through his thick hair.

"Caroline. Wedding bells. Pink balloons."

"Pink," he said. "Anne, promise me you'll never wear pink."

"I'm making no promises to you." She grabbed his arm as he swayed. "Except to take you home."

"Not to New York." As her eyes adjusted to the dimness, she could see that his shirt collar stood up rakishly. He reminded her of a buccaneer or a swordsman from a silent film.

"Excuse me?" she said as he swayed again. She hoped they weren't both going to tumble into the rosebush.

"Not home to New York," he said.

"I have good news. You live in Chicago," she said. "Now can we please get down before we fall?"

"Your wish is my...whatever." In his noble attempt to assist her, Eric nearly knocked her over.

"You first."

"A gentleman waits for the lady." He stifled a hiccup behind his hand.

"I'm not a lady, I'm a journalist," she said. "Besides, if you ruin my shoes, I'll kill you. Now get down there."

She gave him a push. Unresisting, he bounced off the wall onto a thin grassy strip alongside the road where, despite a stumble, he quickly righted himself. She got the impression that being on solid ground steadied him.

Anne was in the midst of a delicate negotiation downward along the wall's craggy face when two large hands caught her waist. She found herself lifted through the air until she thumped against Eric's muscled torso.

The impact took away her breath. A tingling awareness spread through her at the way their bodies were stretched together from point to point.

Like the vines clinging to the wall, they twined around each other. Their legs interlaced, Eric's sinewed firmness unmistakable through the texture of his slacks and her stockings.

A sense of wonder claimed Anne. She touched Eric's neck and his silky hair, relishing the contact.

His hips and shoulders brushed hers; his male arousal stimulated her yielding center; and his lips grazed her temple, her cheek, her throat. Mouth met mouth, hesitant, hungry.

"Oh, Anne." Eric lifted his head to look at her, then kissed her again, more firmly.

She inhaled his heady mixture of musk and cologne. All male. And every inch not hers.

A tiny sob welled from her. She wasn't sure he heard it. "We have to—" His lips covered hers for a blissful, agonizing moment. "Have to go," she breathed.

"Home." He smiled in the moonlight. "Together."

"Oh, lord." She recalled the knot of people she'd seen camped out in front of the hotel when she drove off. "The reporters."

"Who?"

"The barbarians at the gate." She tried to recall the lay of the land from her previous visits. "There's a service road that runs near your cottage. I'll let you off there if you think you can stumble indoors by yourself."

His eyelids drifted to half-mast. "I thought you said we were going home. Anne, that's not right. Not by myself."

He rocked back dreamily, and the heat between them dissipated. "You're three sheets to the wind," she said. "Isn't that the correct nautical term for someone who gets smashed on a yacht?"

"Only on a sailboat. Yachts don't have sheets."
He leaned on her for support as he swayed. "Except
on the beds. I like beds, don't you?"

"My car is this way." Staggering a little beneath
his weight, she half-dragged him to where she'd left
her sedan. The door creaked as it sagged open.

"I'll get in now." Eric made a feeble motion that
failed to dislodge him from leaning heavily against
Anne.

"You have to crouch or you'll never fit." It would
have been easier to shovel him into the back seat, if
that hadn't been filled with file boxes, a spare cooler,
Genevieve's reserve makeup and hair products, and
of course the scuffed shoes.

"I could drive if you like," he offered.

"I've got enough dents in my fender, thank you."
Propping the passenger door open with her hip, she
guarded his head with one hand and shoved him
backward with the other.

He landed rear-first on the seat, with his legs sticking out. "Too small."

"What would you suggest? A tow truck?"

"A limo," he said. "But it's gone. Anne, I didn't
know I was this—this—blotto."

"Don't apologize," she said. "You're the one
who'll take the consequences tomorrow."

"I think I hit my brother." The remark came out
of nowhere. It reminded her, though, of the scene in
the ballroom earlier.

"Did you throw him off the boat?"

"He jumped." Eric transferred his legs inside, one
at a time, with the assistance of his hands. "If you
stop suddenly, I may need a knee transplant."

She closed the door and went around to get behind

the wheel. "Why did you drink so much? It isn't like you." The ignition choked, sputtered and finally caught.

"I love you, Anne."

The statement was so unexpected that it almost didn't register. When it penetrated, it stirred not an answering tenderness but a spike of anger.

She didn't dare speak. She was too busy trying to steer as he lolled beside her, watching her with melting eyes. She was also too furious to trust herself with words.

They had nearly reached the hotel before she replied. "You picked a fine time to tell me. Not that I believe anything you say in this condition."

"I never say what I mean except when I'm in this condition," he answered ruefully.

"You do this a lot?"

"Never. I mean, never since college."

The hotel's service entrance proved to be mercifully media-free. Anne followed the narrow lane behind the cottages and halted in a parking bay. "That's Ivy Cottage right there."

"I'll be fine." Eric opened his door, tried to exit headfirst and fell onto his hands.

For her own preservation, Anne was tempted to push him clear of the car and drive off. Furious though she was, however, she couldn't leave him crawling on a service road.

After some shifting of weight and stumbling about, they both achieved an upright position and headed for the path.

HE'D TOLD HER he loved her, even though she didn't believe him. It was, Eric felt sure, a step in the right direction.

Steps and directions seemed to be the order of business. Skirting a mud puddle. Following a walkway made lumpy by tree roots. Circling to the front of the cottage.

He dug out his card key and waved it before the lock. A click and they were in.

For some reason, they proceeded through the room in a darkness alleviated only by the glow of a streetlamp shining in the window. Vaguely, he recalled that Anne wouldn't want anyone to see her here. But he needed for her to stay, because otherwise some terrible thing was going to happen tomorrow.

He wished he could remember what it was.

"You're going to have to sleep on the couch." She tried, and failed, to ease his arm from around her neck. "I can't help you up those stairs."

"Too steep." Cottages ought not to come with loft bedrooms. Wall-to-wall mattresses seemed so obvious, Eric wondered why the designer hadn't thought of it.

He sagged onto the sofa, dragging Anne down with him. "Take your shoes off," she said.

"Why?"

"They're muddy."

"Not until you take yours off." It would slow her down if she tried to run away. He had to keep her here until she understood that he meant what he'd said.

He wanted a lifetime of evenings with Anne. Of sitting on stone walls talking nonsense. Of quarrels that could be resolved, followed by lengthy sessions of lovemaking in front of a fireplace.

"Fine." Her shoes plopped to the carpet. "Satisfied?"

Carefully, he dislodged his loafers. He had been afraid they would turn out to be tightly laced sneakers, but they peeled right off.

He tried to remember what he intended to do. Talk? Too difficult. Besides, on a night of revealed truths, how could anyone miss the obvious? Man, beloved woman, couch...

"Ah," he sighed, and pulled Anne on top of him, full-length along the sofa.

"Eric! Let me go!" Her fragrant hair spilled over his throat. She was all softness and elbows, but it would take more than a sharp nudge to dissuade him tonight.

"I love you," he murmured, in case she'd forgotten, and ran his tongue along her jawline.

"Stop that!" When Anne wriggled, her breasts got mashed against his chest. He could feel the hard nubs, and the womanly fullness.

He pressed his nose into the shell of her ear. "We need to straighten things out."

"Darn right we do!" Her hips shifted, stirring arousal. He wanted to join with her so intensely, it was like a beacon in his brain.

"Love me back, Anne," Eric whispered.

"In a pig's eye!"

"Should never—have been parted." There, he'd uttered a complete thought. Almost complete, anyway. "Me, you. We should fix this." Since she still didn't seem to get the point, Eric added, "Now."

"Never!" She heaved with all her might. Since his arms were wrapped tightly around her, they both rolled off the couch and crashed onto their sides on the carpet.

The breath whumped out of him. Eric didn't care. "Stay with me." Lying partly underneath, he couldn't stop touching her hips, the curve of her waistline, the edge of her breast. "It's perfect."

She slapped him. It took several seconds for the sensation to penetrate his pickled brain. "Ouch."

This time, Anne succeeded in untangling herself. "You're the most selfish man I've ever met!" She lurched to her feet.

"Me?"

"Even if you told me you loved me when you were sober, I wouldn't believe you!" she cried. "You're always taking the easy way out, trying to please everybody! How could I ever trust you?"

She didn't understand. Everyone depended on Eric. His brother, his stepsister, his mother, his friends. Above all, Caroline. He was the one they relied on. He would never let them down.

"Don't." He meant to add, "go." The word got lost en route from his mind to his mouth.

"I'm leaving." Anne poked him with one foot. "Move. You're lying on my other shoe." He groped for her ankle. She dodged him. "Forget it. You can leave it at the desk in the morning."

"Love," he mumbled.

"Save it for the altar." A cold emptiness replaced her warmth as she left.

As SHE HOPPED toward her car, Anne could feel steam rising from her ears. How dare that man babble about love when all he wanted was sex!

Heck, he was too intoxicated to know what he

meant. He bold-facedly said he loved her, on the eve of his wedding to Caroline. The worst of it was that, deep in her heart, she yearned for it to be true.

His touch tonight, and her barely restrained response, forced her to admit that she hadn't gotten involved with anyone since their affair because no one else measured up. No one else made her shiver with longing. Or laugh so much, either.

She'd certainly read him the riot act. What would Eric Bellamy, powerful editor and society leader, think in the morning if he remembered her accusation that he was weak and untrustworthy? Well, it served him right, and she wouldn't take it back.

Ahead of her, a white blur shifted into the path. Grabbing a tree branch, Anne barely stopped in time to avoid tripping.

The white cat's eyes glowed. It studied her cautiously before prowling forward to rub her calf.

"Hi." She wished she could bend down and stroke it. One-legged gymnastics had never been her forte, however. "How's life treating you?" The cat mewed plaintively. "Exactly," she said, and watched it meander away.

With her temper dropping to near normal, Anne had to admit she deserved to be in this bind. She'd known five years ago that loving Eric was a losing game. Yet, without meaning to, she'd never entirely given up hope.

Tomorrow afternoon, when she watched him stand at the altar with Caroline and say his vows, she would have to accept the truth, she told herself as she got in the car.

Her cheeks felt wet. It had to be dew, or maybe the sprinkler system. She refused to shed any tears over that man, ever again.

Chapter Eleven

Eric awakened on the floor. He was trying to figure out why men would be pounding on the roof so early in the morning when he realized the noise came from inside his head.

Once before in college, he suffered a hangover. Although he wished he could remember what his fraternity brothers had given him for it, he'd been in too much pain at the time to concentrate.

There must be aspirin in the bathroom. Swan's Folly provided its guests with samples of shampoo, soap, perfume and shower caps. Surely some merciful soul had put a painkiller in there, too.

Sure enough, he found four of something labeled Maximum Strength and took three. That left one. He suspected the math wasn't going to work when this dose wore off. If he could muster the strength, he would have to raid one of the other cottages.

He threw water on his face. Each droplet smarted. The stubble on his chin begged to be removed; thank goodness he had enough sense not to wield a razor while in this state.

Back in the living room, Eric made a halfhearted effort to replace the tumbled sofa cushions. That was when he noticed the slightly flattened red velvet shoe on the floor, the one that matched a permanent indentation in his rib cage.

He picked it up and smoothed it, inordinately pleased to see it return to its proper shape. As he would too someday, he hoped.

Setting the shoe aside with a mental note to return it to Anne, he switched on a small hot-water pot that came with packets of restorative beverages. By the time Eric drank a cup of instant coffee, the pills began to take effect. He was contemplating the merits of a shower when someone tapped at the door.

Hope leaped like a candle flame. Maybe Anne had changed her mind. Maybe she did love him.

If it was her, he would admit that she'd been right to accuse him of caving in to others. In his present sorry state, grouchy and tender in all the wrong places, Eric lacked the energy to deceive anyone, even himself.

He didn't deserve Anne. He'd betrayed her, along with his own soul. And he'd been doing it for years.

Nobody had asked him to play savior to his family members whenever they got themselves into binds. He'd taken that role on himself, and he hadn't even done a very good job of it.

In spite of his efforts, things were a mess. His brother and Bianca quarreling. An incompetent reporter screwing up assignments at *The Loop*. Eric engaged to a woman he no longer understood.

He opened the door and blinked in the daylight. Blond hair, heavily sprayed and wrapped around her head like a helmet. A frilly pink blouse over pink-and-white checked slacks. Cold blue eyes and a tight mouth. Not Anne.

"You look terrible." Caroline marched into the cottage. It was, he reflected, the first time she'd come inside in the three days since they arrived.

He leaned in the doorway, hoping the fresh air would revive him. "You know about bachelor party."

"Yes, I heard you tied one on last night. *Everybody* was talking about it. *My* party was an even worse disaster!" As she paced around the dining room, her finger traced the table in search of dust. If she found any, she didn't say so. "My own mother got up and acted like—like— Well, like *her* mother! If I ever get that dotty, I hope you shoot me."

Eric knew better than to speak, because whatever he said would be wrong. He settled for regarding her expectantly.

From her purse, Caroline produced a couple of sheets of hotel stationery. "I want you to read this."

"Can't you just tell me?" He hoped it was a Dear John letter, although he had the impression those weren't usually delivered in person.

"You said I needed to write a column to prove I can do it. Well, here it is!" She stuffed the papers into his hand.

"Caroline," Eric said, "I can't even focus my eyes this morning, let alone read."

"I stayed up for hours!" Her voice rose half an octave. "My hand hurts from scribbling with a stupid pen. You have to read it!"

Her remarks pierced his swollen head as if a woodpecker were mining it for breakfast. "Okay, okay." With a wave of the papers, Eric staggered to a chair. "I'll do my best."

"I'll wait." She folded her arms and leaned against the table.

Mercifully, her handwriting showed the effects of a rigorous private-school education. Evenly shaped letters marched along like well-drilled soldiers.

Hi! I'm Caroline Lambert Knox Bellamy," it began. "I'm going to be telling you readers some of the neat things going on in Chicago society. As you know, I'm in the eye of the hurricane!

"My cousin Petsy Lambert Thorpe is putting together the fine arts ball this year, and it's going to be spectacular!! Picture this: swans imported from the hotel where I got married in June, swimming on a pond in the middle of the ballroom! There'll be an all-white color scheme except for black masks—we'll be as elegant as swans! Can you wait to see what our favorite dress designers will do with this theme? I can't!"

A few paragraphs later, he lowered the pages. "Well?" said Caroline. "You won't get that information about the ball from anybody else, not this far in advance!"

She was forgetting that, due to the relatively slow process of publishing a magazine, everybody in Chicago would know about the all-white fine arts ball by the time this column saw print. The real problems, though, were her amateurish style and the lack of a sophisticated viewpoint.

"You can tell it was written by an insider, can't you?" Caroline persisted. "Like that reference to dress designers and how they're going to turn themselves inside out whipping up concoctions. They're very competitive, you know. I could do a whole column about them."

"You know," Eric said, "you do have some decent ideas."

"What do you mean?" She pursed her lips. "I don't like the way that sounds."

His head hurt too much for him to placate her, and Anne's accusations rang in his ears. "This column is written in a gee-whiz style that would work great in, say, a sorority newsletter." Eric kept a level tone. "A column in *The Loop* requires a measure of irony, even cynicism."

"I thought I could count on you!" Caroline cried. "Look at all the work I did! If you don't like my style, get somebody to polish it."

"I can't give you a job you're not qualified for," Eric said quietly. "And you shouldn't ask me to."

Caroline stared at him in shock. He felt a little shocked himself at his unaccustomed directness.

"I shouldn't ask you to?" she repeated, pacing into the living room. "Even though I'm going to be your wife, there are things I'm not supposed to ask you?"

"You ought to seek a career in broadcasting, if you want to be in the media," he added. "You have the looks for it, and the connections. If you want to be a writer, you've got to learn your craft."

Caroline stood rigidly facing an end table, her back to him. "Is that all you can say?" He thought he heard her purse snap shut, or maybe that was her jaw.

In his present state, Eric could hardly stand upright, let alone negotiate the shark-infested waters of a conversation with his fiancée. "I can't hire you," he said.

She turned and headed for the door. "Never mind."

Obediently, he moved back. "Never mind?"

"Forget the whole idea. I don't want your help." Tears burned in her eyes. When he reached to touch her arm, however, she jerked away and marched out, chin held high.

Eric hated to hurt her this way. He knew some people considered Caroline to be willful, even spoiled, but he knew a side of her that others didn't. The little girl, lost and alone, who needed someone to cling to.

Maybe she was outgrowing that helplessness. If only she'd done so months ago, they might both have changed their minds about this wedding. But he couldn't abandon her now, virtually at the altar.

A shower, a shave and fresh clothing failed to resolve his dilemma, although they made him feel marginally more human. On the way out, Eric checked around for Anne's shoe so he could return it.

Nowhere in sight. He must have knocked it behind something, and he was in no mood to go prowling under the furniture.

He would have to retrieve it later.

IN THE MIDDLE of applying her makeup, Anne heard two voices, male and female, rise in argument from the Knoxes' suite next door. In the two years she'd worked for Genevieve, it was the first time she ever heard her boss quarrel openly with Hainsworth.

What a disturbing development, particularly on the

morning of their daughter's wedding! About to suffer from empty-nest syndrome, Genevieve needed to get closer to her husband, not alienate him.

Then, as she put away her lipstick, Anne realized that the masculine voice didn't belong to Hainsworth. It was lower and louder, like an old-fashioned orator.

Now she recognized it from the wedding rehearsal. This was the Reverend Horatio Lovejoy, a forceful man who headed a socially prominent congregation. He was, according to Genevieve, a trendsetter in his own way, seizing on the latest ecclesiastical trends with sometimes unseemly gusto.

In the seventies, he'd grown his hair long and introduced rock music to the service. In the eighties, he donned a designer suit and remodeled the sanctuary. The late nineties had brought a call for strict morality, including a demand that young church members sign a vow of premarital chastity.

Anne respected high morals. She was less impressed by people who leaped on bandwagons and might just as quickly leap off.

Whatever the argument concerned, the reverend was drowning out even the formidable Genevieve. Anne didn't hear any comments from Hainsworth, so she supposed he must have gone out to check on the wedding preparations.

The wedding. Her stomach clenched.

Today marked the point of no return. As she slid her feet into her remaining undamaged pair of shoes, she reminded herself that she ought to be glad.

After today, she couldn't fool herself any longer. After today, Eric wouldn't dare make drunken protestations of love. After today, the still-glowing embers inside her heart would crumple and blacken.

In Anne's otherwise well-ordered world, these feelings made no sense. Why should she love a man she didn't trust? How could she still nurture an affection for Eric when he was going to marry another woman?

Her hope was that these irrational emotions would die as unexpectedly as they'd arisen. That she would once again find herself, in old-fashioned terms, fancy-free.

Meanwhile, she could tell by her employer's outraged tone, she needed to effect a rescue. Cautiously, Anne cracked open the door to the suite. Now she could make out the words.

"You can't seriously expect me to toss aside that wedding gown and whip up another one right before the event!" Genevieve was chiding. "Not to mention how much that dress cost!"

"If you had attended my services more often, Mrs. Knox, you would have foreseen this problem," returned the Reverend Lovejoy. "As I've been trying to explain, it is improper for a young woman to wear white at her wedding when she's been openly living with the groom."

"Caroline hasn't been..." Genevieve hesitated. "Well, not openly."

"Do you deny that this couple is having intercourse?" boomed the minister in a voice that probably carried into the next county.

"I don't spy on them, but they've known each other since college!" returned his opponent. "I did once happen to see a packet of birth control pills on Caroline's bureau. At least they're taking precautions!"

"You admit that they're living in sin," he boomed

again, "and yet you would present your daughter to the world as a virgin. That's immoral, Mrs. Knox!"

Anne tried not to think about Caroline and Eric being intimate. Instead, she concentrated on the fact that her boss needed her.

If Horatio Lovejoy really believed it was a sin for a nonvirgin to get married in white, he would have made the point firmly and unmistakably long ago. This smacked of a power play.

Resolutely, Anne slipped into the sitting room. Genevieve, dressed to the teeth for the wedding breakfast, stood fiddling with her pearls. The minister's tall, imposing figure struck a righteous pose before the fireplace.

"Excuse me," she said. "I couldn't help overhearing. Pastor Lovejoy, Caroline's wedding dress was ordered months ago and the design was written up in the newspaper. May I ask why you're raising this issue now?"

"Yes," seconded Genevieve. "I don't understand why you've chosen this late hour to protest."

The minister's face took on a ruddy hue, like a child caught with one hand in the cookie jar. "It isn't exactly the first time I've mentioned it."

"Last month, you suggested trimming the dress with yellow ribbons, or was it scarlet?" snapped Genevieve. "It didn't suit the wedding colors and furthermore, I didn't realize it was meant to be a command from on high."

"I can't go against my own preaching and perform a wedding under these circumstances," he pronounced. "The bride will simply have to adapt her gown so it isn't pure white."

For several years, the man had presided over a

weekly TV show on local cable. Recently, there'd been talk of expanding onto a national cable network. What better way to gain publicity, Anne mused, than by flexing his muscle at the most prominent society wedding of the year?

Genevieve had paled at the prospect of her daughter's special day being disrupted. Anne couldn't let her down.

"Maybe it isn't my place to say so," she told the minister, "but to the best of my knowledge you've conducted no premarital counseling and never asked this couple about their religious commitment. The only thing you seem to care about is what Caroline is wearing. Of course, forcing a last-minute change in her gown would give you something to crow about on the air, wouldn't it?"

Fire flashed from Genevieve's eyes. "This is a publicity stunt!"

"Not at all!" blustered the minister.

"Will you or will you not perform this ceremony as you agreed, with my daughter wearing a perfectly respectable white dress?"

He cleared his throat. "I assure you, it's only a matter of a few ribbons."

"You're fired!" cried Genevieve. "Go!" She pointed melodramatically toward the exit.

The man hesitated, and Anne wondered if he might backpedal. Instead, he strode away.

"I'm sorry," she said when she and her boss were alone. "I spoke out of turn."

Genevieve drooped against the arm of the sofa. "No, you were right. The man is insufferable. But now what shall we do? We must have a minister!"

Anne patted her employer's hand. "The hotel

might have a chaplain on call. Or perhaps one of the guests is authorized to perform marriage ceremonies. It would be like asking if there's a doctor in the house.''

Genevieve brightened at once. ''You can make discreet inquiries this morning.''

How ironic, Anne thought as she fetched her purse before going downstairs. Once again, it was her task to make sure Caroline's wedding took place as planned.

And, once again, she intended to do so to the best of her ability.

As IT TURNED OUT, the task of finding a replacement minister was handled with surprising ease.

When Genevieve and Anne arrived in the morning room, a cozy, plush chamber off the main lobby, a handful of people were helping themselves to food at the buffet. Judging by the thinness of the crowd, most of the guests had either overslept or chosen to skip this event.

Lacking much appetite, Anne selected some scrambled eggs and toast. Genevieve took a bit of everything, then led the way to where her daughter Winnie sat.

Winnie's companion, a young woman with long auburn hair and unusually pale skin, wore a leopard-print sweater and a crushed velvet skirt. The large brim of her feathered hat dipped over her forehead, nearly obscuring her eyes.

''Anne, have you met Saffron Shrempf?'' Winnie asked. ''She's Lizzie Muldoon's partner in that delightful shop.''

The two women exchanged greetings. Anne didn't

recognize the name from the guest list, but the bridesmaids were entitled to bring a date or friend for the weekend, so she assumed Saffron had accompanied her partner.

A moment later, Vivian Bellamy swooped into a seat, her red hair curling gloriously around her shoulders. "Isn't it a splendid day for—whatever?"

Genevieve regarded her counterpart severely. "My dear Vivian, as the mother of the groom, you should be made aware that our minister has departed unexpectedly. Do you know whether any of the guests is qualified to take his place at the ceremony?"

"I am!" said Saffron. Her seatmates regarded her with varying degrees of skepticism. "Honest! I've presided at several weddings."

"You have the proper credentials?" Genevieve asked dubiously.

"Of course!" In the shadow of her hat, the young woman's face assumed a serious air. "I don't believe it's enough to be a businesswoman. A person needs to develop her spiritual side."

"Yes, but..." Absently, the bride's mother fingered the tablecloth. "You don't strike me as the ministerial type." Her gaze seemed to linger particularly long on the leopard-print sweater.

"I assure you, I'd be properly dressed for the occasion," Saffron said. "Frankly, I'd love to make a contribution to this event, after all you and your family have done for our shop."

"It's a lovely idea," said Vivian. "Someone of their own generation, who operates on the same wavelength. What better person to join Eric and Caroline?"

Genevieve gritted her teeth, as if she could think

of quite a few better persons. None of them, however, happened to be hanging around Swan's Folly on this particular day. "I suppose it would be all right. By the way, what *is* Eric talking about so earnestly with your friend Lizzie?"

Startled, Anne turned in her chair. She hadn't seen Eric come in.

His head resting on one hand, he was indeed engaged in conversation with the dark-haired bridesmaid at a small table. He didn't notice when Caroline swept into the room, frowned at him and marched to her mother's table.

"Coffee. Black," she ordered a waiter. "I'm not having anything else. I couldn't possibly eat!"

"What's wrong, dear?" Genevieve asked. Saffron and Vivian regarded the bride with interest.

"I don't trust him!" cried Caroline. "I don't trust any man!" She burst into tears.

"But Eric's so cute!" said Winnie.

"Perhaps their auras aren't properly synchronized," offered Saffron.

"You've got a case of cold feet," Vivian said. "Believe me, my son is so dependable, he's boring."

"Look at him, having a heart-to-heart talk with that—" Caroline stopped. "Where did they go?"

The table where Eric and Lizzie sat moments before was now empty. Anne couldn't spot either of them in the room. Those two seemed to have a talent for disappearing.

"I haven't seen Bianca this morning," Genevieve added. "Where do you suppose she is?"

Anne couldn't bear to sit here for another second. She knew Eric wasn't involved with either of those bridesmaids, yet she couldn't reveal that fact without making a long and embarrassing explanation.

He'd probably returned to his cottage to work on the article. Several reasons sprang to mind why she needed to go after him. To press her demand for a joint byline. To find her missing shoe.

"Would you like me to drop by his cottage, Mrs. Knox?" The formal mode of address seemed appropriate in front of the others. "I could ask if he has any last-minute letters for me to type."

It was Caroline who spoke. "Yes, why don't you? You haven't got anything important to do anyway. The rest of us need to get dressed for the wedding. And, Anne!"

"Yes?" She folded her napkin onto the table.

"If you find anything…compromising, you come and tell me at once! Do you understand? At once!" The bride's voice rose, hammering home the point.

"If anything's changed, it should be your fiancé who tells you," Anne said softly. "I'll make certain that he does."

Weighted by conflicting emotions, she left the room. The truth, she realized, was that she wanted to see Eric one more time before she lost him forever.

Chapter Twelve

Usually, Eric could count on his old friend Lizzie to cheer him up. Today, however, she'd changed from the wide-eyed admirer of their college days into a woman with an edge.

She'd told him point-blank not to get married unless he wanted to spend every spare moment with Caroline for the rest of his life. That it would be kinder to leave her now than to expose them both to a disintegrating marriage.

But Eric knew Caro better than Lizzie did. Despite his fiancée's newly revealed ambitions, he could still see her fragility.

On his way back to the cottage, he could have sworn that the earth's gravity had doubled overnight. It wasn't entirely due to his hangover, either. He was coming to terms with his own doubts.

Nevertheless, a decent man wouldn't expose his bride to public humiliation because of his own change of heart. He had to go through with this ceremony and attempt to work things out with Caroline. It was even possible, once she experienced the physical side of love, that their relationship would deepen.

A part of him didn't believe it. But he had to give her every chance.

The sound of hammering startled him. For a moment, he feared his hangover was intensifying despite a plentiful infusion of coffee and cholesterol. Then he noticed the workmen swarming over the grounds.

A white-draped altar stood before the crumbling mock castle, with arrays of pink and white roses being placed so as to define the seating area. Off to one side billowed the pink-and-white striped fabric of a massive tent for the reception.

He couldn't cancel the wedding now. The new Eric, the one he was determined to become, did what was right, regardless of how much it hurt.

He felt his spirits lift at this noble resolution, until he spotted Monty DeLong lingering outside Ivy Cottage, his blond hair matted and his pouty face unshaven. "What's the matter?" Eric asked when he came closer.

"Oh, there you are! Thank goodness!"

Eric took out his card key. "Is there some problem with the wedding coverage?" Then he noticed the suitcase and the laptop computer at Monty's feet. "What's this?"

"I thought you might let me move in," said the reporter. "My room is intolerable, and you'll be in the bridal suite tonight. Why shouldn't I have the cottage?"

The man had a point, Eric conceded. "Come back in a few hours and I'll see what I can do. I'm busy right now."

"I've checked out of my room and there's nowhere else for me to go," Monty said. "I simply couldn't get ready for the wedding in that pit.'' He waited expectantly.

For once, Eric didn't bother with diplomacy. ''You can shave and change in the men's room, like a real reporter. You're here to do a job, not pamper yourself.''

From the young man issued a gasp. ''You're forgetting who I am! I'm not some social nobody.''

''You're my employee, that's who you are,'' he said. ''By the way, that article you wrote on dating services was inaccurate and libelous. I had to bring in a more experienced reporter to fix it, and I'm giving her a joint byline.''

Until this moment, Eric hadn't known what he planned to do about Anne's credit. He only skimmed the story, but it was clearly a professional job.

As he awaited a reaction, it occurred to him that the young cub might resign. He doubted he would get that lucky.

''If you take away half my credit, I'll sue!'' was the unexpected response.

''For what?'' he asked.

''Every cent you've got!'' Resentment twisted Monty's narrow face. ''My Dad's a lawyer, remember? I'll get *The Loop* away from you!''

Although tempted to enumerate everything he'd done to help Monty, Eric knew it would be useless. Besides, he'd lost his last shred of patience. ''Not only can I well afford to hire my own lawyer, but I'll make sure everyone in the publishing business learns what an incompetent, ungrateful twerp you are.''

Monty's stunned expression put Eric in mind of a

popped balloon. Apparently he'd been bluffing. "Well, I guess I won't..."

"One more thing," Eric said. "You're fired."

"But—the wedding!"

"We'll run photos only. A picture is worth a thousand words, remember?" He went through the door and closed it in Monty's face.

Through the curtains, he watched as the young man trudged away with his head lowered. An urge to call him back and give him another chance died half-formed. Not after that ugly threat of a lawsuit.

Journalism wasn't an appropriate career for the kid, anyway. He needed to get into a field where people could succeed on looks, ego and connections. Maybe politics.

Eric frowned as another movement caught his attention. Someone was heading toward the cottage. Anne.

She gave Monty a puzzled look as he brushed by, then resumed her course. Eric wished he could soothe away that troubled expression. If only, one more time, he could hold her and tease her and see merriment light her face.

Releasing the curtains, he took a firm grip on himself. He had to live up to her high standards, even if she wasn't likely to appreciate the sacrifice.

MONTY DIDN'T LOOK HAPPY. Anne supposed that might be a good sign, but at this point the issue of her credit in *The Loop* hardly mattered.

Eric admitted her before she could knock. "I saw you coming."

"Trouble with the troops?"

"I fired him," he said. "It was long overdue. Also, I'm giving you a joint byline."

She clasped her hands together and discovered they were damp. "You liked the story?"

"I've only skimmed it, but it looks good," he said.

They stood so close she could tell he'd forgotten to put on cologne. He didn't need it; he radiated a subtle, potent masculinity.

She wanted to touch that dark hair and those high cheekbones. She ached to stand on tiptoe and stretch her arms toward him, and feel him move forward until they came together. It wasn't even sexual. It was a recognition of something profound that existed between them.

Not sure what to say next, she prowled toward the couch. "I came to get my shoe."

"It must have fallen behind something," he said. "I saw it this morning but then it disappeared."

"Shoes don't move by themselves." She refrained, however, from accusing him of kicking it out of his way. A man in the throes of morning-after-the-bachelor-party-itis could be forgiven a bit of testiness.

Crouching, Anne felt beneath the couch. The hotel staff did no better a job of cleaning there than they had under her bed, she discovered when she retrieved a nest of dust along with one paper clip, part of a dry-cleaning receipt, and a fossilized piece of hard candy.

"No luck," she said.

Eric checked behind an end table. "Not here."

She peered under an upholstered chair. He examined the corners of the room. Nothing.

"Maybe the maid took it," she said.

"While I was showering? I don't think anyone came in." He shook his head, then winced. "Sorry, I'm still a bit under the weather. I'm sure it'll turn up."

Anne supposed she ought to be upset, since she spent so much on the shoes, but she couldn't take her mind off Eric. How vulnerable he looked this morning and yet, conversely, how distant. As if he'd matured last night.

Had something happened after she left? "Caroline was upset this morning," she said. "Not that it's any of my business."

"But you're dying to know?"

"Reporter's instincts." That wasn't true. "Actually, I noticed that you're different this morning. I thought there might be a connection."

"Different how?" In the morning light, his eyes glowed a clear amber.

"You gave me a byline even though it might make waves. Then you fired Monty, which will create even more trouble." She nibbled at her lip before continuing. "There's something different about the way you hold yourself, the thrust of your jaw. Even the way you run your hand through your hair."

He removed his hand, which had indeed just finished disarranging his hair. "I do that differently?"

"You're more contained," Anne said. "There's less wasted motion." He'd altered, subtly but unmistakably, from a youth to a man. "You've grown up."

"You must be the most observant person I've ever met." He started to smile, then sobered quickly. "The fact is, I'm committing your words to heart."

"Which words?"

"About taking the easy way out," Eric said. "That

I try to please everybody, and that makes me untrustworthy. You were right.''

''I know,'' she said, smiling.

He gave her a rueful grin. ''You're not going to soft-pedal the blow, are you?''

''You don't need soft-pedaled truths.''

Eric didn't bother to argue. ''In answer to your question about Caroline, this morning, she brought me a column she'd written. She wants me to make her an editor on *The Loop*. I said no.''

''That could explain why she seemed so distraught at breakfast,'' Anne agreed. It wasn't the answer she'd been hoping for, however. ''There wasn't—anything else?'' *You didn't tell her that you love me?*

''Not that I know of.'' His eyes grew hooded. ''Anne, I'm going ahead with the ceremony unless Caro chooses to cancel it. We've come this far together. I have to see it through.''

He *had* grown and changed. There was a tilt to his head, a new determination in his gaze; an awareness of his own power, but also a kind of resignation. Was it possible he'd come to terms with the fact that no one's life, not even his, was guaranteed to be perfect?

Maybe Anne's comments had helped him. How ironic that the person who would reap the benefit of that growth was going to be Caroline.

It took a moment for his next words to sink in. ''Now that I've given Monty the boot, there's an opening on my magazine. The job is yours if you want it.''

She'd almost forgotten, in her confusion about their relationship, that Eric could single-handedly jump-start her career. He was offering her a plum position.

"We can't work together," Anne heard herself say. "It isn't wise."

"It wouldn't be easy," Eric corrected, "but we could handle it."

"Maybe you could, but—" She stopped. No way would she admit how deep her feelings ran, not when he loved her so little. "Sooner or later, people will find out that we worked together in California, and that could raise some awkward questions about why we didn't mention it earlier. I'd never want to make trouble between you and your wife. I will take that recommendation you promised, though."

"You'll get it," he said. "Nevertheless, I hope you'll reconsider about the job. I think we can handle the fallout."

Not trusting her voice to hold steady, she shrugged and left. The sense of having forgotten something important dogged her down the path, until she remembered the velvet shoe.

She would have to go back and search for it later. Much later, when the cottage was empty of everything except memories.

On closer reading, the article confirmed Eric's impression of Anne's skill and professionalism. She'd spliced in the changes seamlessly while retaining the best of Monty's quips.

Offering her the job had been an impulse. The right impulse, Eric didn't doubt.

What would it be like working together again? At this point, he was in no shape to think that far ahead.

After making a few minor changes in the article and altering the byline, he E-mailed it to Gabby Greer at the magazine. In his accompanying note, he mentioned that he'd fired Monty and would hire a replacement as soon as possible.

Outside, he heard footsteps and then a crisp knock. For once, Eric, who usually enjoyed being the life of the party, wished people would leave him alone.

If it was Neill, he would tell the truth about Bianca, right after he apologized for taking a swing at his brother on the boat last night. In the light of day, he felt fairly certain that flying fist had belonged to him and not some unseen deckhand.

When he admitted the new arrival, however, he found himself facing the unhappy countenance of his future father-in-law. Dire possibilities pounded through Eric's aching head: Caroline had thrown a tizzy fit about not becoming an editor. Monty had threatened to sue over his hole-in-the-wall room. Or—?

"Sorry to disturb you," said Hainsworth, "but we're having a little trouble managing the press."

"You mean DeLong?" he asked. "What's he threatening to do now?"

The hotel executive's forehead creased. "I didn't realize there were any problems in that regard. I was referring to the ones still occupying our front driveway."

"Oh, the *real* press." Eric massaged his temples. "Do you happen to have any aspirin on you?"

Hainsworth handed over two shrink-wrapped pills. "We've had a lot of requests for those this morning, so I stocked up. If you don't feel like dealing with the reporters—"

"Just give me a minute."

After downing the pills, running a comb through his hair and checking to make sure his face wasn't too puffy, Eric accompanied Hainsworth toward the front of the hotel. En route, he learned that the minister had been canned at the last minute, giving rise to all sorts of speculation. In addition, a couple of paparazzi were reputedly scheming to crash the ceremony.

"My wife already arranged for a substitute minister," Hainsworth said. "She claims there was some misunderstanding about the wedding dress, which doesn't make any sense to me, so maybe we should leave that out."

"I'll make some general comments, crack a few jokes about the bachelor party and promise that Caro and I will make an appearance before the reception so they can take their pictures," Eric said. "That should hold them."

"You're sure you don't mind?"

"Not at all." He would much rather face a horde of pesky reporters than Caroline in a bad mood, although he would never say so to her father.

Besides, Eric relished the chance to keep busy. The last thing he wanted to do in the next few hours was listen to his own doubts.

CONTRARY TO WHAT Caroline might believe, Anne had plenty to do today. She fetched replacement cosmetics from her car for Genevieve, double-checked last-minute details that nagged at her employer's peace of mind, and reassured her that Eric showed no signs of ditching his bride.

"I do hope my daughter will be happy," Genevieve said as she munched on some appetizers she'd ordered from room service. "She needs a good marriage."

"Who doesn't?" Despite having eaten little at breakfast or lunch, Anne lacked an appetite. At least she wouldn't have to worry about going on a diet after this weekend.

"Caro more than most," said the bride's mother. "People don't like her much, you know. She has a thousand acquaintances, but no real friends."

Surprised, Anne studied her employer. "But she's such a social leader. Everyone admires her."

"Caro has a hard time getting close to people. She's a very private person," Genevieve said. "I can't help thinking it's partly my fault."

Anne reached over to pat her hand. "Parents shouldn't blame themselves for everything."

"Yes, but we made a serious mistake." Genevieve folded her hands in her lap. "When Caro was ten, Winnie broke her neck in a car accident. Fortunately, there was no paralysis, but she had to have several surgeries. Instead of dragging Caro back and forth to the hospital or leaving her with the housekeeper, Hainsworth and I sent her to boarding school."

"I should think that would have encouraged her to make friends," Anne said.

"It made her lonely," Genevieve said. "But she was too proud to complain. In fact, she stubbornly stayed away for four years; I think she was miserable, but in a way she wanted to punish us."

"How self-defeating."

"Oh, Caro's like that," sighed her mother. "Once she gets hold of something, even if she doesn't really want it, she hates to let go. I think loneliness is like that. Sometimes I've wondered if it isn't true of Eric, that she doesn't stick to him partly because she's afraid to be without him. But this marriage will be good for them both. They're such a lovely couple, aren't they?''

Anne managed a slight nod and decided to change the subject before she blurted out her real opinion of the forthcoming marriage. "And you look stunning yourself."

The older woman grimaced into the mirror at her silvery-blond pageboy. "I ought to try a new hairstyle, don't you think?"

"Not today!"

Genevieve laughed. "You have a talent for cutting to the point! No, I didn't mean today. Next week, perhaps. Heavens, with the wedding over, I'll have so much free time." She sounded sad rather than pleased.

Anne wished she could say something consoling, but she had her own demons to wrestle with. As soon as she could find a pretext to leave, she wandered down to the lobby, relieved to be alone even in the midst of a crowd.

People were assembling in their wedding finery although it was only the middle of the afternoon and the ceremony didn't begin until six. Florists carted in so many large arrangements that Anne couldn't imagine where they would put them all. Amid the hubbub, a swan from the pond even wandered inside and was chased noisily away by a porter.

Four-year-old Lambie Thorpe, wearing a tuxedo for his role as ring bearer, scampered between people's legs. "Lambie? Where are you, cutie poochy?" called Petsy Thorpe, wandering about in her bridesmaid's gown.

Privately, Anne didn't see how the women could bear paying huge sums for the overblown pink dresses Caroline had chosen for them. If she had a more cynical nature, she might suspect the bride of having purposely outfitted them in the ugliest possible style to make herself look more beautiful.

Then she froze. Through the activity waded a smartly dressed Monty DeLong, his face newly shaved with a Band-Aid on one cheek and his blond hair tied back in a ponytail. When he took no notice of her, she realized with relief that he didn't even know that she was the one who'd rewritten his article.

He headed straight for Petsy, who had seized her wriggly son and was trying to wipe a dirt streak from his forehead. "Mrs. Thorpe!" he cried. "I've had the most splendid idea!"

"About what?" Petsy asked distractedly.

"The fine arts ball!" Monty said. "What you need is a publicist with an inside track on the media. Frankly, I'm tired of this tacky business of being a reporter. Why don't you hire me?"

"That's an interesting idea." The society matron clamped on to her son's arm as he made another getaway attempt. "Lambie, do hold still, little tootsie-wootsie! You know, Monty, I'm concerned about my dress for the ball. Can you believe most of the designers are already booked, six months in advance?"

"The problem is the all-white theme," Monty said. "If the guests aren't careful, they'll end up looking like a gaggle of over-the-hill brides."

"It was Caro's idea. She insisted on it or she wouldn't come." With a sigh, Petsy released her son. Instantly, Lambie shot through the crowd and vanished. "He can't get too lost, can he? Anyway, I think she's planning to have her wedding dress short-ened and the bow removed; it should look smashing, but what about the rest of us?"

"You could always order out of a catalog," joked Monty.

"A catalog!" Petsy beamed. "I could find some-thing at The Velvet Fig. Those Victorian dresses in their catalog are darling! Did you see the samples?"

Anne didn't hear Monty's response. The discus-sion about clothes had made her think about the sim-ple beige sheath with a beaded jacket that she herself was wearing. She'd found it at a thrift shop and had to sew most of the beads back in.

It had been cut for someone a few inches taller, so it didn't hang quite right, and the fabric had yel-lowed in several places only partially hidden by the jacket.

Caroline's high-handed advice came back to her. *Until you learn to go after what you want, you'll never be anything but my mother's secretary.*

It was too late to go after Eric. At thirty-one, how-ever, Anne hardly considered herself—what was Monty's arch term?—over the hill.

Eric might feel obligated to marry a woman whom Anne doubted he loved with either joy or passion. She, however, still had a chance to find Mr. Right.

A man who made her laugh and who sent wild impulses raging through her body whenever he lev-eled his smoky gaze at her. A man she could love as much as she loved—used to love—Eric.

She would never find him by blending into the woodwork. Last night, she'd been right on target when she bought those velvet shoes. Now she needed to make another change.

Did she have time to run out to a dress shop? Could she possibly hope, on such short notice, to find an outfit spectacular enough to announce to the world that Anne Crumm was seizing the day?

That was when she swung around and ran into Lizzie Muldoon.

"Oops!" The dark-haired bridesmaid, not yet dressed for her duties, regarded her with friendly concern. "My gosh, did I hurt you?"

"No, I don't…think so." To her surprise, Anne's voice trembled. She hadn't realized she was nervous. Or excited. Or both.

"Anne, I don't mean to pry, but is there anything I can help you with?" Lizzie asked.

For once, fate was playing into her hands. The co-owner of The Velvet Fig, the very woman that Petsy Thorpe planned to consult about her fine arts ball gown, was offering to help.

"Yes." Anne inhaled deeply and plunged onward. "I keep hearing about all the beautiful dresses you brought this weekend. I'm really sick of plain suits. I don't suppose you'd have anything I could wear to the wedding tonight?"

"Wow." Lizzie stepped back and examined her eagerly. "I love makeovers!"

"I'll pay, of course."

"Never mind that!" The beaming girl waved away her offer. "Genevieve's one of my investors, you know, and you've done a lot for her. I've brought tons of samples; it's good for business."

"I—well—thank you." Anne wondered how the other guests and her own employer would react if she decked herself out prominently at the wedding.

She had to take chances if she planned to get ahead, though, didn't she?

"Come on, let's go up to my suite!" Lizzie steered her to the elevator. "I have all kinds of things that are going to look great on you!"

Anne hoped she was right.

enough to the bride and groom," said Clarise, relenting with a hard in direction. "Unfortunately, I had to kick the artist out. You wouldn't believe what a too this place was! People standing in and and... With the floor out of them.

"Why did you have so many people in there?" Anne gazed in delight at the palette of green. She felt an impulsive to... the bold ... strokes and to every fiber ... ... with her own hands at the woods... that the fleeing one. "That ...

Chapter Thirteen

The Velvet Fig co-owner whisked Anne to the suite she was presumably sharing with her partner, the minister-to-be, although there was no sign of Saffron. "Just let me grab some things and we can start!" Without waiting for a response, Lizzie dashed into a bedroom.

Considering that the elegant suite had been occupied since Thursday, its classic furnishings showed remarkably little clutter. Puzzled at smelling varnish, Anne peeked into the master bedroom. A half-finished painting, apparently intended to show the bridal couple, leaned against the bed.

The artist had captured Eric in startling detail: the humorous quirk of his mouth, the boyish openness of his gaze, the rebellious lock of dark hair on his forehead. Only a faint sketch suggested the face of the bride beside him, however. It might, Anne reflected, have been anyone.

She wondered if the painter would see the changes in Eric this morning, were he to pose for finishing touches. The new reserve, the hint of regret. Or was she the only one who could detect them?

"That picture was supposed to be my wedding

present to the bride and groom," said Lizzie, returning with a load of dresses. "Unfortunately, I had to kick the artist out. You wouldn't believe what a zoo this place was! People running in and out... Well, I've taken care of that!"

"Why did you have so many people in here?" Anne gazed in delight at the jumble of gowns. She got an impression of crushed-velvet fabrics and tapestry prints that would go splendidly with her new shoes, if she could find the missing one. "These clothes are unbelievable!"

"Thanks. Saffron and I select everything ourselves," the bridesmaid chattered as she arrayed her wares across a sofa. "As for why we had such a crowd, Budge Bellamy's one of our backers and he simply wouldn't believe that two women could run a business without masculine assistance, so we, er, let him believe I had a fiancé who was involved. Well, somehow I ended up with *two* pretend fiancés, the painter and Saffron's airhead brother. He's the stripper who jumped out of the cake at the party, a real gold-plated idiot. They were both such a pain, I threw them out."

Anne tried to sort through the stream of information. "So you're not really engaged? Genevieve seems to believe you are."

"No, although I've finally met someone I could fall in love with. At the wedding, can you believe it?" Lizzie studied Anne, muttered something about her coloring and began riffling through the clothes.

"Does he—this man you've met—know about your pretend fiancés?" She wondered if it was one of the groomsmen. However, if her hostess didn't choose to reveal the man's name, it seemed impolite to ask.

"He knows they're fake and he wants me to tell everybody the truth, but I'm afraid it might hurt the shop. We had kind of a sharp disagreement on the subject." Lizzie held up a blouse with leg-of-mutton sleeves. "This forest-green would bring out the shade of your eyes, don't you think?"

Anne stroked the fabric. "It's lovely. Not quite what I had in mind, though. I'd like something more romantic."

"Sure. If you're going to change your image, why not go all the way?" The dark-haired bridesmaid tossed the blouse on the couch. "Anyone in particular you're trying to impress?"

Anne caught her breath and searched frantically for an acceptable reply. "This hotel is bursting at the seams with good-looking men, from the groom on down."

"You know, I had a crush on Eric Bellamy for years." Lizzie prowled around the sofa, examining the rest of the wares. "I introduced him to Caroline in college, and she stole him. Right under my nose!"

"You must not have minded too much. You're still one of her best pals or you wouldn't be a bridesmaid."

"Actually, I was surprised when she asked me to be in the wedding." Lizzie held up, then rejected a black velvet skirt and a ruby sweater. "Do you think they're happy together, the bride and groom? I don't. I think she's entirely wrong for him, which makes me feel guilty because I brought them together, even though I didn't intend to."

"You think they're unhappy?" She was half-afraid to explore the subject, yet unable to restrain herself.

"Happy people don't fight all the time," the young woman said briskly. "Besides, she's so…" She wrinkled her nose and threw up her hands in a fair imitation of Caroline's hysterics at the party the previous night. "And he's so…" She assumed a dreamy expression.

"Do you still have a crush on him?" Anne couldn't resist asking.

"Oh, no! That's completely over." Lizzie selected an Edwardian dress covered with cabbage roses. "How's this? No, too busy. I just want Eric to be happy. But I don't suppose you know him very well. I hope I'm not boring you."

"Not at all." Anne didn't like keeping this friendly woman in the dark. On the other hand, she could scarcely get a word in edgewise, so lengthy explanations were impossible anyway.

"This might work. In fact, I think it's perfect." Lizzie handed her a dark-red velvet gown. "Try it on!"

Anne caught her breath. It matched the shoes, the ones she didn't have. That hardly mattered, though; she loved this dress on sight, even if she had to go barefoot. "It's stunning."

"Use my room," the young woman said. "There's a pile of accessories, so take what you need. How about a hat? Or a black velvet purse? Help yourself!"

Anne couldn't believe how generous Lizzie was. It almost made her think better of Caroline, to know she had a friend like this, except that the bridesmaid had said the two of them weren't close.

As she went to change, Anne remembered what

Genevieve had said about her own daughter. That people didn't like her much.

For the first time, she felt sorry for the bride. The woman seemed to have everything, including Eric, but not even her bridegroom showed much eagerness for her company, and her own bridesmaid considered the two of them ill-suited.

In spite of everything, Anne admitted silently, she would never want to trade places with Caroline Lambert Knox.

ERIC WAS SURPRISED at how easily he placated the press, although he suspected the more enterprising among them were merely biding their time. In any case, everyone seemed to buy his story that the minister had been called away on an emergency. The other questions, while irritating, proved manageable.

No, he and his bride hadn't spent last night together. They were, he said, anticipating a traditional honeymoon, and he would leave the rest to their imaginations, thank you.

Yes, his brother Neill and stepbrother Joe had indeed fallen off the yacht during the bachelor party, but neither was any the worse for wear. As for rumors that the bachelorette party had turned into an orgy, he assured them that all the ladies remained as intact as they'd ever been, which brought a few chuckles.

In answer to another query, he confirmed that he had fired the reporter from *The Loop*. Yes, he responded to several simultaneous inquiries, he would be taking applications when he returned from the honeymoon.

Eric smiled into the blinding glare of lights, thanked everyone and departed with Hainsworth.

"Fine job." The man shook his hand. "You're a good man. Make sure my daughter doesn't run you ragged."

It seemed an odd remark. "Run me ragged?"

"I'm afraid we've spoiled her," Hainsworth said glumly. Even in late middle age, his symmetrical features and full head of hair still made him a handsome man. "She's used to having things her own way."

"I'm sure we'll get along." Eric hoped he would survive this marriage as well as his father-in-law had survived his own. Although Hainsworth and Genevieve might not act like lovebirds, they had stayed married for thirty years, which was quite an accomplishment.

After he and the older man parted company, he edged through the busy lobby to the bar. In contrast to Thursday night's noisy scene, he found it almost empty.

"What'll it be?" asked the bartender as he took a stool.

Eric had no desire to risk drinking alcohol again anytime soon. He wasn't even sure how he would manage to toast his bride with champagne in a few hours. "Club soda."

The man poured a glassful and left Eric to contemplate the bubbles.

The scents of aged wood and fine liquor infused the dark-paneled room. Its deep silence and its dimness after the afternoon glare eased Eric's tension.

A stocky figure entered and headed toward him. "How's the head?" boomed Budge Bellamy, not the least subdued despite having drunk more than his share at last night's party.

"A bit fuzzy, Dad," he admitted.

"What're you drinking, vodka? Make sure you have three or four. Just think, two more hours and you're no longer a free man!" chortled his many-times-married father. "Temporarily, anyway." To the bartender, he said, "Whiskey and soda."

Eric wasn't sure he could handle a father-son talk just now. His father spoke mostly in exclamation points, and rarely listened to the response. Important messages had to be shouted.

Besides, he could hardly expect his dad to understand his inner turmoil. Budge's attitude was that if one marriage didn't work, he just moved on to the next one. As an adolescent, Eric had resented him bitterly, and since then his feelings had mellowed only somewhat.

Viv—he rarely thought of her as Mom since she'd become an artist—and Budge had divorced when he was six, remarried when he was twenty, and divorced again four years later. Most of his childhood had been spent with Neill and their single mother, except for holidays with his father and whichever step-mother, stepsiblings and half siblings were currently in the nest.

"Dad?" He raised his voice to make sure he got his parent's attention. "Do you ever wish you'd stayed married to the same woman all these years?"

"The same woman?" repeated Budge. "And break the hearts of my other wives?"

"What about their broken hearts when you left them?"

"Mutual agreement! Mostly," said his dad. "Besides, if I'd stayed with your mother, I wouldn't have Fawn and, uh, let's see. My other son.''

"Kevin."

"Right! Kev!" Budge downed a mouthful of Scotch. "Life is to be lived, kid. You love 'em, and when it fades, you go for the gusto!"

"You sound like a beer commercial," Eric said.

"Beer, God bless it." Budge patted his tight gut. "I steer away from the stuff, but it does sell pretzels!"

To his surprise, Eric no longer resented his father's heedlessness toward the pain he'd inflicted on his former wives and his children. The anger that had lingered for so long was gone.

Maybe it was because Eric now understood how complicated life could be. Sometimes you had to choose between one kind of pain and another.

"So you're happy with Rhonda?" he asked. Having a stepmother two years younger than Eric himself had been a blow at first, especially since she displaced Vivian the second time around. He cherished his little half sister, though, and Rhonda tolerated Budge's self-indulgences much better than her predecessor had.

"Sure!" said Budge. "Maybe this one'll stick. You never know!" After finishing his drink, he regarded his son intently, which was so unusual that Eric began to wonder if he had something hanging from his nose. Then Budge said, "You know, I'm proud of you, son. You've made a name for yourself."

"With your help." Not every aspiring publisher had a father who could lend him start-up capital.

"You paid off the loan, though." Eric waited for

any additional comments, but none was forthcoming. Apparently Budge had given as much fatherly praise as his nature allowed.

"Guess it's time for me to go put on my tux."

"I still fit into mine from two weddings ago. No, three." The pretzel king pushed away his empty glass. "Ursula D'Alessandro was a beautiful woman. Only lasted two years, though."

"I know." Eric scarcely remembered Bianca's mother. Her main achievement was bringing his stepsister into the family. "Well, Dad, I'll see you at the ceremony."

"Keep the penguin suit," Budge said.

"Excuse me?"

"The tux," he said. "That's my advice to you, son. Always have a penguin suit ready. You never know when you'll need it."

"I suppose I'll be wearing it to the fine arts ball." Sliding from the stool, Eric shook a cramp out of his leg.

"Or whatever. Keep it handy or you'll regret it—take my word." His fathered waved him on his way.

ANNE DIDN'T PUT her new dress on until the last minute. She might soil it, the way she had to rush about the grounds with a clipboard as an increasingly tense Genevieve demanded she double-check one preparation after another.

Fortunately, Hainsworth had everything well in hand. He seemed amused and tolerant of his wife's anxiety rather than resentful.

At four o'clock, Winnie, Bianca and Petsy gathered with Caroline in the large salon of the bridal suite to pose for photographs. Lizzie remained conspicuously absent.

"Where do you suppose Elizabeth has gone?" Genevieve demanded. "She should be here for the final festivities! Look how cute the girls are, posing with Caro. How dare she miss this?"

Anne considered suggesting they check the bridesmaid's suite, until she remembered that Lizzie had met a man she liked this weekend. What if the two of them were in a compromising position? It would be a poor way to repay the woman's generosity.

Besides, no one was having any fun, least of all the bride. From her tightly upswept blond hair to her pinch-toed satin heels, Caroline formed a picture of discomfort. A wedding gown, Anne thought, ought to be soft and sensual, not so stiff it could double as a cage.

Finally, at about five-fifteen, she was sent to her employer's third-floor suite to fetch some pressed powder. It was time, she decided, to change out of her suit.

When she put on the velvet dress and regarded herself in the mirror, she saw that it had an almost magical effect. Anne's complexion smoothed, the line of her neck lengthened and her eyes grew larger. Even the tired black pumps she'd been rambling around in all day didn't hurt any more.

She doubted that, like Lizzie, she would be lucky enough to meet Mr. Right during someone else's wedding. Still, she was in a sense making her debut as a post-Eric eligible woman. And she liked what she saw.

She hoped Eric would like it, too. Not that it mattered, of course.

When she descended to the second floor, however, no one in the bridal suite noticed Anne's transformation. Of course, that might be because everyone was in a flurry of last-minute prepping.

The bridesmaids gathered their bouquets. Caroline grasped an array of pink and white flowers so exotic that Anne feared some of them might be man-eating.

Downstairs, the lobby had cleared out. They swung through a side entrance to avoid being seen by the guests and slipped around the building toward a striped tent.

As if nature understood that Saturdays in June were meant for weddings, it graced them with mild late-afternoon sunshine. On the deep-blue pond, swans glided picturesquely.

"How beautiful," Bianca murmured.

"So romantic!" cooed Petsy.

Anne scarcely heard them through the pounding of her heart. Her hands were so damp the clipboard kept sliding away.

Although she'd been helping to plan this event for a year, her sense of resignation disappeared and grasshoppers rocketed about in her stomach. In half an hour, Eric would be married.

Forever tied to Caroline. At least, it might as well be forever. Anne wasn't foolish enough to waste her life waiting for a married man to come to his senses.

Far off, she heard the rhythmic *whump* of a helicopter. "Oh, dear!" Genevieve gazed skyward. "You don't suppose those horrible reporters are up to something, do you?"

The noise faded. "Maybe we've been spared." Anne's mouth felt so dry that her tongue stuck to her palate.

"Looks like the prodigal child has arrived." Petsy pointed toward a bewildered-looking Lizzie emerging from the back of the hotel.

"At last!" Striding across the lawn, Genevieve grabbed the bridesmaid by the arm and yanked her into the tent. "You come in here right now!"

"I thought the wedding was at six," protested Lizzie. "I'm fifteen minutes early, aren't I?"

"You were supposed to be in the bridal suite two hours ago!" snapped Genevieve. "Anne? Anne? Where are Elizabeth's flowers?"

"Right here," she said, handing over the tightly bound bouquet.

Lizzie clutched the beehive-shaped arrangement without seeming to notice it. Escaping Genevieve's grasp, she peered through a slit in the tent at the guests. Who was she looking for? Anne wondered. Had there been another quarrel with that Special Someone?

"Elizabeth! Get in line behind Bianca," Genevieve commanded.

"Excuse me." The bridesmaid scooted toward the open tent flap. "I'm really sorry. There's something I have to do."

"Stay here!" Caroline's mother grabbed for the bow wriggling on the bridesmaid's rear end, and missed. "Anne! Bring her back!"

For a moment, Anne froze. She hadn't intended to make a dramatic entrance in front of the whole assembly in her low-cut, look-at-me dress.

"Hurry!" said her boss.

Wordlessly, Anne handed over the clipboard, lifted her velvet skirt and skimmed out of the tent into the sunshine. Then she paused to catch her bearings.

Lizzie had taken a stand in the center aisle and was making some kind of announcement. The guests twisted and angled in their white fabric-covered chairs to get a better view.

"I need to tell you that I am not and never have been engaged," the bridesmaid declared. "To anyone."

She peeked toward one of the groomsmen. Eric's stepbrother Joe, that was the guy, Anne decided. He returned Lizzie's gaze for one flicker of a moment, then resumed his remote expression.

Apparently this display of conscience was for his benefit. Anne hoped it paid off for Lizzie.

Near the altar, Eric stood riveted. Not by Lizzie, though. He was staring directly at Anne. His gaze slid from her heated cheeks down her throat and along the scooped neck of her gown. Hunger burned in his eyes.

Her skin got so prickly she could hardly breathe. Nerves tingled in her breasts and thighs, and her ankles went weak.

She must have been kidding herself about selecting this dress for some imaginary Mr. Right. She'd worn it for Eric. For heaven's sake, he was a groom waiting at the altar for another woman. How could she have made such a fool of herself?

Lizzie retreated toward the tent. Somehow, Anne found the strength to follow.

She scarcely noticed that, in the distance, the *chop-chop* of the helicopters had resumed.

AFTER THE LONGEST year of his life, after a weekend that had become an adventure in self-discovery, after a headache-ridden morning that seemed like it would never end, time was playing a trick on Eric.

It speeded up so abruptly that nothing seemed real. How had he landed so suddenly at the altar? How had all these people assembled without his noticing?

The only thing that anchored him was the sight of the woman in the cranberry velvet dress, her chin held high, her hair falling in a bell shape around her face. He wished she would walk up the aisle toward him. He wished he could reach for her hand and murmur reassurances into her ear.

Then she fled after Lizzie. Instinctively, Eric took a step forward, until he caught a quizzical look from Neill. He coughed and pretended he'd simply lost his balance.

Lost his balance? He must have lost his mind. This whole wedding was a huge mistake.

Until this moment, the impact of what he was doing hadn't fully penetrated. The entire event had taken on such overtones of a Hollywood production that it overshadowed the fact that, despite their wealth and position, he and Caroline were simply two human beings who planned to spend the rest of their lives sleeping and eating together, holding and supporting each other, growing old in each others' arms.

How could he make this commitment when his heart belonged to someone else? But how could he betray everyone's trust, right here at the altar?

Dazedly, he noticed a short woman in a screaming yellow dress and an oversize hat taking her place on the podium. This must be the substitute minister. Where on earth had Genevieve found her?

Hope flared within Eric. This had to be a dream,

a crazy vision from which he would awaken any minute now. It couldn't happen soon enough.

INSIDE THE TENT, giggles greeted the sight of the yellow-clad pastoress when she became visible through the open flap. Fawn and Lambie, who had been produced by Rhonda a few minutes ago, poked each other until they nearly toppled over.

"Who's that?" Petsy asked.

"Saffron," said Winnie. "Lizzie's partner."

"What church is she ordained in?" asked Bianca.

Genevieve took Kevin's arm as he prepared to lead her to her seat. "She has performed many marriage ceremonies."

"I certainly hope so." In place beside his daughter, a tuxedoed Hainsworth straightened his bow tie. "Although I must admit, I can't imagine what church would hire her."

"It's the Cloister of the Goddess of Universal Bliss and Sunshine, or something like that," Lizzie volunteered. "They're into spreading joy. I think all the members of the Cloister of the Goddess perform ceremonies, actually. They get those mail-order certificates, to make it legal."

Genevieve blanched. "Did you say...*goddess?*"

"We'd better go, Mrs. Knox," said the usher, and led her gently away.

"I hope she'll be all right." Hainsworth seemed more concerned about his wife's state of mind than his daughter's. Beneath her veil, Caroline hadn't moved a muscle. She scarcely seemed to care who was officiating.

A harpist began to play. Thank goodness for wedding rehearsals and for Petsy, a veteran of several such ceremonies. She prodded the flower girl and ring bearer to depart on cue, followed by the bridesmaids.

Anne would have preferred to remain out of sight. Better yet, to retreat to her room. Hainsworth, however, had a different idea. "Anne, why don't you go out there and reassure my wife about this goddess business? I'm sure we'll all laugh about it someday."

"Of course." She made her way out the other side of the tent so as not to appear part of the procession. There were indeed seats empty beside the bride's mother, and she took one.

Genevieve didn't so much as glance in her direction. Neither did anyone else as the harpist segued into "Here Comes the Bride" and Hainsworth stepped into view with Caroline.

Chapter Fourteen

An alarm clock would have been nice. Anything to awaken Eric from this dream that was rapidly degenerating into a nightmare.

He'd never seen Caro so tense; she tromped down the aisle like a robot. When she reached him, she ignored him. Even Hainsworth studied her with concern before releasing his daughter to Eric.

As for the lady minister, she bypassed the traditional "Dearly beloved" for "Welcome, cherished spirits of light and goodness!" She went on to proclaim a mystical union and a mingling of souls.

He *had* to be dreaming. Only one thing struck him as undeniably real: the ever-louder *whirr* of a helicopter, or perhaps two or three of the darn things.

"Caroline!" the pastoress yelled over the noise. "Do you take this man, Eric, as your lawful wedded soulmate, to nurture and support, to cherish and encourage, to give roots and wings, in harmony and in unity, so long as your souls shall inhabit this mortal plane?"

A long pause fell over the lawn, the congregation, the swans, even the helicopters. After so long a preamble, had the bride forgotten the question?

"Caroline?" prompted the lady in yellow.

"Say it!" cried Genevieve.

At last, Caro came to life. She pushed back her veil, turned to face her gathered friends and relatives and, in a voice loud enough to steer ships through a thick fog on Lake Michigan, bellowed, "No!"

BESIDE ANNE, Genevieve went rigid with shock. From a few seats over, Nana Lambert's voice demanded, "What did she say?"

Anne couldn't believe what Caroline had done. From the startled expression on Eric's face, it was obvious he hadn't expected it, either.

"What! Why?" Genevieve demanded of no one in particular. "She's so close to success! Why throw it away?"

"Because she's so unhappy," Anne said. "Look at her."

Tears streamed down Caroline's cheeks. Everyone stared openmouthed.

With visible effort, the bride pulled herself together. Above the hubbub of the copters, she declared, "I refuse to marry him because he slept with her last night!" Slowly her finger traced the line of bridesmaids, or maybe she was indicating the front row.

Anne felt as if everyone must be staring at her. Of course, she hadn't slept with Eric last night or Thursday night or any night in the past five years, but that didn't mean she hadn't wanted to. Or that she hadn't participated in some stolen and highly unethical embraces.

She wasn't the only one who believed herself the target of the bride's wrath, she learned when Lizzie spoke up. "Me? He didn't sleep with me! I was with Joe."

In the line of ushers, Eric's stepbrother nodded cautiously. "It's true."

The finger trembled as it continued to aim accusingly toward... "Don't look at me!" cried Bianca.

Standing beside Eric, Neill took a deep breath. "I can vouch for where she was last night," said the best man. "All night."

"Really?" Eric clapped his brother on the back. "Good for you! That is— Caro, wait a minute—"

"Look at him!" screeched the bride, not at all dissuaded by these denials. "He doesn't even bother to deny it!"

"Deny what?" the groom asked in bewilderment. "I was so drunk last night I passed out on the floor of my cottage."

The wind from the helicopters whipped Caroline's veil and made the nearby tent walls flap like sails in a hurricane. Anne and the other ninety or so guests leaned forward, straining to hear.

"Then how do you explain this?" roared the bride, as she yanked something from beneath her enormous bouquet.

Amid the clamor, no one else seemed to grasp what it was. But Anne recognized it. She knew Eric did, too.

It was her missing shoe.

CAROLINE MUST HAVE spotted the shoe when she visited him this morning, Eric realized. In retrospect, he recalled hearing her purse snap shut while she was standing with her back to him.

The situation was so outlandish that, if it hadn't

been so awkward for all concerned, he might have laughed aloud. While he'd been determined to deny his love for Anne and do the right thing, some imp of fate had misled Caroline into forcing his hand.

However, neither her mistake nor her wild accusation let him off the hook. He had to figure out how to calm things down and get on with the business at hand.

Caro didn't give him the chance. Instead, she flung her bouquet at her mother and stormed down the aisle, trailed by a dazed Petsy. Anne caught the flowers just in time to prevent them from hitting Genevieve in the face.

The guests arose and shuffled about as if unsure whether to wait for Caroline's return or flee for their lives. The little flower girl and ring bearer scampered about gleefully, screeching amid the excitement.

A helicopter swooped so low Eric could see late-afternoon sunlight glint off a camera lens. It hung around the neck of a man who leaned out of the doorway and then, in what seemed like slow motion, launched himself into space. A collective gasp arose from the onlookers.

As the man plummeted, he fiddled with something on his chest. A ripcord. A harness. Dear lord, the numbskull was wearing a parachute, but he wasn't nearly high enough for the thing to inflate.

"Go back!" screamed Nana.

The man hit the sloped roof of the tent, bounced and landed in a cloud of white atop Lizzie Muldoon. Joe raced toward them.

His stepbrother Joe, the fireman, could do a far better job of rescuing the duo than Eric could. Caroline, who paid no attention to the havoc behind her, was disappearing into the hotel.

He had to talk to her. He had to explain about the shoe, and bring his bride back to the altar.

With a heavy heart, he went after her.

WHEN SHE SAW Eric run in pursuit of Caroline, Anne's last hope shriveled. All he had to do was tell the truth and the wedding would proceed as planned.

"I can't stand it!" moaned Genevieve.

"Me, either." Anne spoke with equal despair, although for different reasons.

"You darling girl! You're always so concerned for others!" said her boss. "Who would have believed Eric would turn out to be such a Benedict Arnold?"

Anne couldn't bear to be the recipient of undeserved admiration, nor to hear Eric abused unfairly. "That was *my* shoe," she said.

Genevieve frowned. "The one my daughter was holding? But I've never seen it before."

"I bought them last night on my way to the lake." Since further explanation appeared to be called for, she added, "It fell off while I was trying to help him onto the couch, and then I couldn't find it. Caroline must have spotted it and jumped to the wrong conclusion."

As the helicopters retreated and the parachutist rose shakily to his feet, Hainsworth turned toward them. "I hate to break in, but we have to make some decisions about the guests and the reception."

"Tell everyone to sit down," Genevieve replied. "The wedding will take place in a few minutes, as soon as the children smooth out this ridiculous misunderstanding."

"I hope not," said her husband.

"What?" asked Nana, joining them. "I can't understand what everybody's talking about! Who's that funny-looking man in the parachute? Is he one of my fans?"

"Come on, Nana." Winnie came alongside her grandmother. "Let's go get a closer look at him, okay?"

"Such a lovely girl." Her grandmother patted Winnie's hand. "One of my finest young dancers." They strolled away together.

With the whirlybirds gone, the guests stood around talking in subdued tones. Anne didn't realize how painfully loud the noise had been until she noticed a residual ringing in her ears.

She also heard Genevieve's piercing question to her husband. "What do you mean, you hope not?"

Hainsworth spoke guardedly, so others wouldn't hear. "Caro's been miserable this whole weekend. I like Eric, he's a fine young man. But if people aren't suited to each other, it's best they find it out early."

"Are you talking about them or us?" Genevieve's voice quavered. It was the first time Anne could recall seeing such a vulnerable expression on her employer's strong-boned face.

"Us?" repeated her husband. "Whatever gave you that idea? Honey, I could never love anyone else."

"But you—I thought—" Genevieve hesitated. "Oh, dear. I suppose this isn't the best time for a tête-à-tête, is it?" She gestured toward the guests and the wedding party, who were milling about uncertainly.

"Let's go have our party." Hainsworth's smile radiated affection. "We've got food and music and you know what? I think you and I may have something to celebrate, after all."

"We couldn't possibly!" said Genevieve. "Not with Caro's wedding ruined!"

"Our friends and relatives have come a long way," her husband pointed out. "The food is here, and so is the orchestra. Furthermore, you and I have a thirtieth anniversary coming up in three months. Let's make the best of the situation and have our party early. Then in September, we can take a wonderful trip somewhere romantic, just the two of us."

"Oh, I would love that! If you think it's all right." Happiness trembled in Genevieve's eyes.

"Go for it," Anne whispered to her boss. She'd been longing for something like this to happen. Although she still didn't understand why the two had drifted apart, she hoped they were off to a fresh start.

"You have yourself a good time, too!" replied her employer. "No more clipboards today!"

Hainsworth stood on a chair and announced to the crowd that they were going ahead with the reception. At his signal, waiters carted trays of food into the tent, and the guests followed.

Would the bride and groom mend their differences and go ahead with their union today? Anne wasn't eager to find out.

The more she thought about it, the more convinced she became that Eric had turned to her because of his dissatisfaction with Caroline. Whatever he felt for her, it certainly wasn't love.

She found herself walking up the slope toward the hotel, in no mood for refreshments or dancing. What she wanted was to pack as quickly as possible and drive to her small apartment in Chicago.

Next week, or when Eric returned from his honeymoon, she would remind him about his offer to write a recommendation. Once she had it in hand, she could resign her position and depart for California. After all, Genevieve had Hainsworth by her side now and Eric's letter would give Anne a head start toward a new job.

It would be nice if Eric returned her shoe, though. Anne might not be able to afford another pair for a while.

PETSY USHERED Eric into the bridal suite. "Talk to her!" she commanded. "And I swear, if you did what she thinks you did, I'll flay you myself!"

"I didn't," he said.

"Go tell her that," said the bridesmaid. "Meanwhile, I'd better find out what my son has done with the ten-thousand-dollar wedding ring."

Eric hoped Neill had had the sense to pocket the thing. He'd hate to lose it, if only because the money could do a lot of good for some worthwhile cause. Besides, he might need it; he still had a duty to try to salvage this situation.

Until now, he hadn't realized quite how enormous this suite was. The salon could have doubled as a ballroom, although several clusters of couches made it resemble a lobby. Floor-length white draperies and the pastel furniture gave it a disconcertingly antiseptic air. How could anyone have a rip-roaring wedding night in this place?

The bedroom door opened one inch at a time.

When Caro came out, he saw that her face was damp. Apparently she'd splashed it with water.

"About the shoe—" he began.

"You want it back? Here!" Snatching it off a table, she flung it at him. The red velvet made a bright contrast to the sterile surroundings as it flew toward him. "Keep it, and your little playmate, whoever she is! If it wasn't one of my bridesmaids, she's obviously a nobody, which is exactly what you deserve!"

Eric caught the slipper and, lacking a pocket to stick it in, held it behind him. "Caroline, calm down." The woman believed she had cause to be angry, he reminded himself, although this whole matter could have been resolved if she'd asked him a straight question this morning. "You're getting carried away over nothing."

"Nothing? Obviously you think a man's entitled to have a fling on his last night as a bachelor!" Rage contorted her features. "Especially if he isn't getting any you-know-what from his fiancée!"

The accusation stung. "I've always respected your decision to remain a virgin until our wedding night," Eric told her.

"Who said I was a virgin?"

"Excuse me?" All thought of explaining about the shoe vanished from his mind.

"You think I've been waiting for you all these years, don't you?" Caroline smoothed down her voluminous skirt. "Well...well...I haven't!"

Was she confessing to some girlish indiscretion? Eric knew he had no right to judge her. "You mean, somebody in high school?"

"No!" she said. "The year before last, when we broke up and I was dating another guy."

"Why him and not me?" Eric said.

"He said he loved me," Caroline returned.

"So did I!"

"Yes, but you said it out of kindness, not passion," she replied unhappily. "Only I found out later that he didn't really love me. He told me I was too clingy and immature."

"So you came back to me?" Eric said. "Why?"

"Because I could depend on you." Caroline sniffled.

"But you're not in love with me. You don't even desire me physically."

"I don't know what that means, being in love." She sighed. "We were the perfect couple and we belonged together. Or that's what I thought until I discovered how you humiliated me last night."

"It's Anne's shoe." He brought it from behind him.

"Who?"

"Anne Crumm, your mother's assistant," he said. "She drove me back from the lake and I fell on it while she was helping me onto the couch. I'm a hard man to budge when I'm soused, so she left without it."

The fight whooshed out of Caroline as it dawned on her exactly what kind of fool she'd made of herself in front of her friends and family. And that she'd flung at him the deep dark secret that she'd no doubt intended to keep hidden.

Her petal-pink mouth worked but no words came out. Eric couldn't help feeling sorry for her and yet, after this revealing conversation, he no longer felt obligated to marry her.

Nor, he thought, did she need him to. "You

know," he said. "You're a stronger woman than you think, Caro. You're perfectly capable of pursuing a career, if that's what you want, and of standing on your own. Why should you settle for a marriage that neither of us really wants?"

"But how will it look?" she cried. "What will the press say?"

"If that's your biggest concern, you don't need me, just a good press agent to put the right spin on things," he said. "Caroline, I wish you the very best in whatever you decide to do next. And I hope someday you find out what love means."

He exited with the shoe in his hand.

ANNE TIGHTENED the cap on her toothpaste and inserted it into a plastic zipper bag. Her shampoo, conditioner and mousse went into another bag. Everything fitted neatly inside the flowered travel case that Genevieve had given her last year when they flew to Texas for her cousin's twentieth anniversary bash.

Outside, an orchestra was playing a Strauss waltz. Inside, the wedding scene replayed itself in Anne's brain.

Saffron, garbed in yellow, spouted mystical nonsense. Caroline shouted "No!" and produced the slipper from beneath her bouquet. The paparazzi paratrooper landed atop Lizzie in a cloud of white silk; it was lucky the bridesmaid hadn't been seriously injured.

What would the press make of all this? Anne wasn't sure how much the photographers had seen or heard. Of course, any good publicist would declare that the intrusion of the chutist was what had broken up the ceremony. If the marriage was called off, some excuse could be devised later.

Either way, it didn't concern her, Anne told herself as she folded a blouse and inserted tissue paper into the creases. She would be moving on.

In the hall, a man's footsteps paced along the carpet. She hoped Hainsworth wasn't going to try to persuade her to join the festivities.

There was no knock. Instead, her door simply opened. "You ought to get in the habit of locking this thing." Eric's impish smile made Anne's heart leap.

His deep-brown hair retained its shellacked bridegroom perfection. The bow tie was askew, however, she noticed with an odd sense of detachment. "Did you and Caroline sort things out?"

He quirked an eyebrow. "No, we called it off. More or less by mutual consent. I came to tell you that we're having a sort of contest here at the hotel."

"What kind of contest?"

He angled into the room. His mischievous grin reminded her of yesterday morning, when he sneaked in with a breakfast tray. "A mysterious princess disappeared from our ball, but she left this behind." He held out the missing shoe.

"Thanks." Anne reached for it.

He snatched it away. "Not so fast. It's my job to make sure it fits."

"Eric, this is silly."

"Humor me." He indicated a chair at the dressing table. "Have a seat, mademoiselle."

Anne plopped onto the tapestried cushion and kicked off her bedroom slippers. "Of course it fits. It's mine."

"How remarkable." He knelt before her. "A number of other young women have made the identical claim but they've proven to be imposters." The shoe got stuck on her left foot. "Wait a minute. It doesn't fit."

"That's the wrong foot."

"Thank goodness." Onto her right foot it went. "Perfect. It must be size—what is this? Triple Z? Never mind."

"Oh, get up before somebody sees you." Her face hot with embarrassment, Anne shifted her foot away.

"There's something else I'm supposed to do while I'm down here," Eric said. "Now let me see. I'm on one knee. What does that suggest?"

Not even the world's most unromantic woman could mistake his intention. But it was wrong, utterly wrong.

"No!" Anne said.

"No?" The joy vanished from his face. It hurt her to see the disappointment.

"I don't mean no, exactly," she amended.

"Then it's no, as in, yes?" he queried hopefully.

"Eric, I'm not ready for you to ask what I think you were going to ask," Anne said. "And you're not ready, either."

He rocked back on his heels. "I thought I was."

"It's too soon."

"Can you give me an approximate date of when would be soon enough?" The teasing returned to his tone.

"I don't know," Anne admitted.

Outside, the waltz segued into a Latin beat. "Well, okay." Standing up, Eric brushed off his knees. "In the meantime, there is one thing I'd like to do."

She scooted off the chair to get away from him. "What's that?"

His melting gaze halted her retreat. Had the room filled with soap bubbles, or was Anne becoming light-headed? "Put on your other shoe, Cinderella," he said. "I'm taking you dancing."

Chapter Fifteen

On the rear lawn of Swan's Folly, the tent shimmered with soft lanterns in the rapidly descending twilight. Over the orchestra, Anne heard laughter and the clink of glasses.

"They're drinking my wedding champagne," Eric said as he steered her across the rear terrace of the hotel. "I hope they drain every drop. I've sworn off alcohol for the foreseeable future."

"Would you mind explaining what happened between you two?" she said. "Didn't Caro believe it was an innocent business about the shoe?"

He poked back a lock of his hair and then, reacting to the stiffness, mussed it energetically. "Remind me never to put that goop on my head again, will you? Maybe I should shave it. Would you dance with a bald man?"

"Yes, but I won't dance with one who refuses to answer a direct question," she said.

"Ah." His hand pressed commandingly against the small of her back, brooking no deviation as they turned left, away from the tent. "She did believe me. Unfortunately, before I could make my explanation, she flung into my face the fact that she'd slept with another man."

"Recently?" Anne asked in astonishment.

"No," he said, "but considering that she has never shown the least inclination to go to bed with me, it made a poor impression."

"She didn't sleep with you? How could she resist?" Anne hadn't really blurted such a revealing thought, had she? "Forget I said that."

"I'm having it engraved on my tombstone," Eric said. "By the way, would you please stop trying to veer toward the lights? We're not moths, you know."

"You promised to take me dancing," she reminded him. "The music is thataway."

"The music is everywhere." He escorted her across a footbridge and past the gazebo. They were heading toward his cottage.

"Eric, don't take me literally," Anne said. "Just because I don't understand how Caro could keep you at arm's length doesn't mean I'm volunteering to make up for it."

"What?" His breath tickled her neck. "Are you suggesting I would go back on my word? Dancing I promised and dancing we shall have."

"Vertically," Anne clarified.

"Absolutely vertically, unless we trip over each others' feet, which we've been known to do," Eric reminded her.

They reached the springy ground beneath the willows. Fireflies darted among the trees while, across the pond, glowing lights turned the tent into a fairy-tale setting. Overhead, stars formed swirls across the sky.

The June night lay enticingly upon Anne's shoulders. It seemed only natural that she should be wearing this special dress and the perfect pair of shoes.

Through the air came the melody of "We've Only Just Begun." The lyrics echoing in Anne's mind seemed entirely appropriate. "We're starting over, aren't we?" she asked as the two of them halted on a level patch of grass.

"I hope not." Facing her, Eric curved one arm about her waist. For once, her elbows and knees positioned themselves properly as the two of them started to dance. "I want to go forward with all our memories intact, even the painful ones."

Strong and gentle, he surrounded her with his heat. Drew her close. Moved against her.

"Painful?" Anne blended into him. "I didn't know any of our memories were painful for you."

"Parting," he said, "was not sweet sorrow. It was the pits. Never again, Anne."

His grip tightened and his cheek rested against her hair. They wove around tree roots and over rocks; they sent an unseen squirrel, or perhaps it was a chipmunk, chittering up a trunk; they inhaled the scents of moss and night-blooming flowers.

The jumble of sensations infused Anne with summer madness. For this eternity, suspended in starlight, she could love Eric fully and freely. She stopped worrying about what might come, how it might end. Or whether it ever would.

As song followed song, they waltzed to the shoreline. The pond's shimmering surface mirrored the moon and stars and tent. A few pale swans glided through the kaleidoscope of lights.

Eric lowered his head and their cheeks touched.

As his hips rocked sensuously, she matched him rhythm for rhythm until they vibrated in unison.

Their lips met. Cool at first. Tentative. He had a hard mouth, but it invited her in with a flick of the tongue.

Points of fire blazed through Anne. She lingered against Eric, tasting his mouth while her body undulated with growing abandon. This dance belonged to her. This man belonged to her, too, at least for one evening.

When he drew back to gaze at her, his eyes filled with wonder. Then a groan tore from deep inside and he crushed her to his chest. She felt the urgency of his need, rivaled by her own.

Stumbling a little as they held on to each other, they scrambled to the cottage. The loft bedroom lay crowned by a skylight. Through it, the moon bathed them in silver.

"I want to see you. All of you." Reaching behind Anne, Eric unworked her zipper in one fluid motion. The velvety dress fell away, and she stepped out of it and the shoes at the same time.

In the coolness, she shivered until his mouth found the pulse of her throat. As he bent over her, he loosened her bra and took her breasts in his hands and then in his mouth.

The aching buds hardened between his lips. When the pressure intensified, Anne clung to Eric, dizzy from the onrush of sensations.

She could barely summon the presence of mind to fumble with his tuxedo jacket. Reluctantly drawing back, he shrugged out of it, ripped off the bow tie and helped her undo the waistcoat, the cummerbund, the cuffs and the starched shirt.

They struggled to coordinate their efforts, pausing here and there for a kiss on bare flesh and a chuckle at their efforts. How impossibly romantic it seemed, this united battle against his stubborn attire.

"I'll never wear clothes again," Eric vowed when, finally and gloriously nude, the two of them tumbled onto the bed.

"They'll tease you about it at the office," she murmured, running her palms over his thighs.

"It'll be worth it." With easy power, he lifted himself above her, pinning her lightly, tantalizing her nipples, her soft core and her lips.

When he entered her with a series of lightning thrusts, the pleasure amazed her. Eric was everywhere, dominating her. Filling her. Loving her.

She gave him back thrust for thrust, and reveled in his eager moans. The passion that rocketed through him reached her as strongly as her own.

Anne scarcely saw the explosion coming before it carried her away into a world that contained only her and Eric—sweaty and brilliant and infinitely happy in a tangle of sheets.

IN THE NIGHT, he awoke. The cool air raised bumps along his skin and he took one last, longing gaze at Anne's beautiful shape before drawing the covers over them both.

How could so much have changed in the space of one day? Eric wondered. He hadn't earned this reversal of events. He didn't deserve to be lying next to Anne, the woman he'd always loved. He would definitely take her, though. Tonight and every other night, if she would let him.

She was wrong if she believed he had proposed

on the rebound. Or that he wasn't ready to make their relationship permanent. However, he could understand if she needed time to sort out her emotions.

It was important to get a grip on his eagerness, Eric supposed. Not to push her too hard. He knew that she loved him. Now he had to give her the chance to accept that he loved her, too.

He sighed and curled around her, spoon-style. Patience had never been his strong point.

THE SUN WOKE Anne early, beating on the skylight with all its summer vigor. Too late, she realized they should have closed the shutters.

On the other hand, she didn't want to sleep in. In fact, she realized as she sat up groggily, there would be a lot of explanations to make if she didn't manage to sneak back to her room unobserved.

"You aren't leaving, are you?" Eric's hooded eyes watched her as he brushed the hair away from her face. "You know, I kind of miss the way you used to wear it, so long, it was like a curtain."

"I'm thinking of shaving it off," Anne teased, echoing his own words from last night. "Would you still make love to a bald woman?"

"Sure, in the dark," he said.

She stood up, tantalized by the awareness that he was watching every movement. "I have to get back before Genevieve notices I'm gone. If she hasn't already."

"I thought you were planning to get back into journalism anyway," he said.

Anne scooped up her clothes. "Yes, but how awkward! I do care about her feelings. And just think…you were supposed to marry her daughter yesterday."

"You have a point." Eric stretched his magnificent body against the sheets. "Although it's too early in the morning to be logical, in my opinion."

She didn't respond. Last night, time had stood still and the future hadn't mattered. Today, she wanted more. And wasn't sure how to ask for it.

When she came out of the bathroom fully dressed, Anne said, "The brunch begins in an hour. I suppose most people will stagger in for something to eat. It'll be awkward but we both ought to make an appearance. Separately, of course."

"I'll see you there, then." Sitting up, Eric pulled her to him for a brief kiss. "Mmm. Any chance we could come to the brunch naked?"

"Highly unlikely."

He fell back against the pillow, blissfully relaxed. She hoped he would add something about getting together later, but he didn't.

She let herself out of the cottage. Across the pond, workmen were collapsing the striped tent. Bits of paper and petals and popped balloons littered the lawn, although she knew these would soon be removed.

Anne was passing the gazebo when she realized she'd been listening for the sound of footsteps. For Eric to come racing up and fling himself at her feet and demand that she marry him.

Instinctively, she wrapped her arms around herself. That was what she yearned for, that he would love her so madly that he couldn't wait. Was he ever going to raise the subject of marriage again? Had last night's lovemaking dissipated his passion?

As she approached the main hotel building, however, she sneaked a guilty peek toward the windows of the second-floor bridal suite. Was Caroline still there? What must she be thinking?

Anne couldn't believe that a woman could be engaged to a devastating man like Eric and not want to possess him physically. Or that she would marry someone she didn't crave in every corner of her soul. Maybe an ordinary person like her simply didn't understand the heiress. Or perhaps Caro didn't understand herself.

Taking a side staircase, Anne made it to the third story without running into anyone she knew. Breathing a prayer of relief, she opened the door to her room.

There stood Genevieve, wearing a mint-green pantsuit and an expression of dismay. Her gaze raked Anne's outfit from the low neckline down to the tell-tale shoes that had made such an impact at yesterday's ceremony. "Well!"

What was the point in denying the obvious? Taking a deep breath, she said, "It didn't happen Friday night but it did happen last night."

Genevieve blinked. "It?"

"Eric and I worked together at a magazine in California and had a brief...involvement," Anne said. "It was all over five years ago. I swear, I didn't sleep with him this weekend and he had every intention of marrying Caroline. My shoe really did get left in his cottage by mistake." She stopped to catch her breath.

"You were at Eric's all night?" Genevieve said, as if she hadn't quite grasped the rush of words.

Anne nodded.

"Well, thank goodness," said her boss. "I was worried when I found you hadn't come in. You should have left me a note. Or called, or... Well, I guess you couldn't have, could you? And if you had, I wouldn't have answered. I was rather busy myself last night.''

Then Genevieve did something for the first time in the two years Anne had known her. She giggled. It was the merry, conspiratorial giggle of a woman who had just experienced a passionate encounter of her own.

"You were busy with Hainsworth?" Anne said. "Congratulations!"

Genevieve perched on the edge of the bed. "Not Hainsworth—Johnny. Hainsworth is his middle name. I thought it sounded more elegant. I used to call him my Johnny, and that's still who he is.''

"You two have been estranged for a long time.'' It was an opening for the older woman to discuss the subject, if she wanted to.

And she did. "Twenty years. Since I was pregnant with Winnie,'' Genevieve admitted.

"Twenty years!'' With only a moment's hesitation, Anne plucked one of her old suits from the closet and began changing into it. She couldn't attend the brunch like this and she didn't want to interrupt the conversation by disappearing into the bathroom.

"I don't mean we haven't, well, done *anything* in twenty years,'' Genevieve said. "But it hasn't been the same as it used to be.''

"Why not?'' It was a nosy thing to ask, but this seemed to be a time for confidences.

"While I was pregnant the second time, a friend of mine told me she heard Hainsworth—Johnny— flirting with a young woman at the country club,'' Genevieve said. "So I watched him, and I could see that he *was* attracted to the girl. It came at a time when I was sticking out to here with the baby, and I felt like a whale.''

"He had an affair?" After running a brush through her hair, Anne applied lipstick. Today, her cheeks were so bright and her eyes so shiny that she didn't need other makeup.

"No," Genevieve said. "But I knew that in his heart he wanted someone else. That I wasn't attractive to him anymore. He was unfaithful in spirit.''

She had wasted all these years of closeness because of jealousy? "I'm sure in a lifetime, everybody gets tempted a few times," Anne said, although she couldn't imagine wanting any other man if she had Eric. "It's whether we yield to temptation that counts."

"I know that now." Genevieve grinned. "I'm calling him Johnny from now on. And you know what? He's going to call me Ginny again!"

"I'm so pleased for you." On impulse, Anne donned her new shoes. So what if they looked a bit dressy for the suit? "I've hoped for a long time that you two would reconcile.''

"It's partially my fault, I suppose," Genevieve continued, her face thoughtful. "About Caroline."

A lump stuck in Anne's throat. It was a touchy subject, although the older woman didn't seem perturbed by it this morning. "What about her?"

"She told me last night that she never slept with Eric," said Caro's mother. "She tried to act as if she had a perfect right to go hypersonic—no, ballistic, isn't that the term?—over that silly shoe. But I saw birth control pills on her bureau once so I know she's no angel. Johnny's right. The two of them simply aren't compatible, and it's a good thing they found out in time.''

Anne hadn't expected to get off this easily. She was delighted, less for her own sake than because she wanted to spare her employer. "But the wedding meant so much to you."

Standing up, Genevieve straightened her slacks. "I've done way too much living through my daughters. Especially Caroline. Well, she's off for New York already...she left late last night. Some nonsense about getting ready for her publishing party and intending to make her mark."

"She might surprise us yet," Anne hazarded to suggest.

"Or learn a few overdue lessons in humility," Genevieve said.

After a knock, Hainsworth poked his head into the room. "I hope you ladies are hungry. The chef laid out quite a spread for this morning."

"We're raring to go!" His wife went to him with such a blissful expression that Anne wouldn't have been surprised to hear her purr.

"How about you, Anne?" said the hotel executive.

"Sure. I'm starving," she said, although she suspected the next hour was going to be about as uncomfortable as any situation she'd endured. At least Eric would be there. At least she could look at him, even if it were from a distance.

Chapter Sixteen

Birds belted out their songs as Eric strolled across the sun-dappled hotel grounds. Why hadn't he noticed before how blue the pond was? And how charming that tumbledown Folly looked?

He loved Anne and he was free to pursue her, as soon as she would allow him to. What more could a man ask on a bright Sunday in June?

How about not to run into Monty DeLong? He broke his stride at the sight of the blond ex-reporter standing on the walkway talking into a cell phone.

Spotting him, the young man hung up. "Well!" he said. "You certainly look cheerful, considering what happened."

"Did you find a place to sleep last night?" Eric asked.

Monty tossed back his long hair. It had been washed recently, which was a blessing. "Caroline let me have the bridal suite after she left."

"She left?"

"First she told me the whole story." The young man was practically preening himself in his white suit. "How you wouldn't let her have a career because you're afraid of the competition, and how she's going to establish herself in the New York publishing industry.''

Eric decided not to bother setting the record straight. "Is that what the news organizations believe?''

"Of course," Monty said.

"How do you know?''

"Caroline and I gave a press conference on the front steps last night." A smug smile accompanied this revelation.

"You what?'' He wasn't sure whether to be amused or outraged.

"It's a wonderful angle," Monty gushed. "A woman discovers her true self at the last minute and leaves her domineering groom at the altar. She's practically a heroine.''

"I see," said Eric.

"After I clear up a few details in Chicago, I'll be joining her in Manhattan," Monty said. "As her personal publicist. I had considered working for Petsy on the fine arts ball, but that would only be a temporary job. This is *much* better.''

"You and Caroline should get along fine," Eric observed dryly.

The young man glanced toward the open French doors of the morning room. "I was planning to have a bit of brunch, but I think I'll pass. The sooner I get home, the sooner I can leave for New York.

"Congratulations. It sounds like you've landed on your feet.''

"I'm just getting started!" Monty said, and strutted on his way toward the front of the hotel.

The kid certainly showed chutzpah, Eric thought.

He hoped the giants of the New York publishing industry had a sense of humor.

He was glad, though, to learn that an acceptable spin had been put on yesterday's havoc. Thank goodness someone had thrown the media sharks a bone, or a guppy, or whatever sharks ate.

With luck, the paparazzi would transfer their attention to Caro's antics in Manhattan. Eric fully expected her to land herself a talk show and possibly come out with a ghostwritten novel into the bargain.

He took a deep breath. He'd lingered so long that everyone else should have arrived at the brunch before him. Now he had to face them en masse.

Taking the terrace steps in pairs, Eric went through the French doors. The hum of voices and the clink of silverware halted abruptly.

He studied the relatives and acquaintances sitting around the English-style morning room. Anne, he noticed, occupied a table with Genevieve, Hainsworth and Winnie.

Joe and Lizzie sat with their arms around each other, obviously in a world of their own. *What was up with those two?* The last time he'd seen them, Lizzie was telling the world she wasn't engaged to anyone and Joe was refusing to meet her gaze. Of course, then there'd been that business with the parachutist, and Joe rescuing her. Now they looked downright cozy.

He saw no sign of the other quarreling couple, Neill and Bianca. They weren't missing much, though, just a lot of wedding leftovers.

In every corner, vases erupted with sprays of pink and white roses. Eric found that the cloying color scheme no longer bothered him.

The centerpiece on the buffet table, though, took him slightly aback. It was a five-tiered wedding cake topped by bride and groom dolls, with Mr. and Mrs. Eric Bellamy written in sparkles around the base. Obviously, someone had forgotten to serve the thing last night. Who could possibly eat wedding cake at breakfast?

"Hi, bro!" hooted Kevin, who had reverted to jeans and a Chicago White Sox T-shirt.

"Hey, Kev!" Eric said. "What's up with Joe and Lizzie?"

"Didn't you hear? They got stuck together in an elevator. All night." Kevin grinned. "Nature apparently took its course. They were even thinking of tying the knot this morning, but Lizzie says they're going to wait to get married at Joe's firehouse with all kinds of family and friends there. So no wedding this weekend, I guess."

"I guess." Since Kevin was such a font of information, he asked, "How about Neill and Bianca? Any word on them?"

"Your mother's been telling everybody they roared off on her vintage motorcycle last night," said his half-brother. "I guess they must have figured out some way to take the baby with them. What do you think? Wedding bells?"

"If I know Neill and Bianca, they'll get married privately without a lot of hoopla," Eric said, pleased to learn the pair had come together at last. "I'm sure it's just a matter of time."

When he looked around, others called greetings: his mother, Nana Lambert, even the Knoxes. The only frown came, oddly, from his father.

"Just get something to eat and let's be done with

this business," growled Budge. "The sooner we all go home, the better."

Until today, Eric would have complied meekly. Now he rejected the chance to slink away. "What's the matter, Dad?"

"You know perfectly well!" flared his father, and turned his back.

"Budge!" said Viv. "Give us all a break!"

Eric's father addressed his ex-wife without looking at his son. "It isn't right not to go through with a wedding once you've announced it! I certainly never would have."

"Even if you had to leave your current wife to do it!" she retorted.

They didn't need a public airing of dirty laundry. "Hey, guys," Eric said. "Please don't fight on my wedding day."

The words slipped out without his realizing it. He heard them at the same time as the other guests, and didn't miss the buzz that resulted. What did he mean, his wedding day?

Judging by their confused expressions, everyone in the room wanted to know. Eric most of all.

He searched Anne's face for her reaction. Anger? Disgust? It was hard to interpret the moisture glinting in her eyes or the way her lips pressed together.

"Who did he say is getting married?" Nana cried into the silence. "Is it that cute paratrooper? I just love a man in uniform!"

He might as well go for broke, Eric decided. No more smoothing other people's ruffled feathers to keep the peace. "I'm going to marry Anne Crumm," he said. "If she'll have me."

Half the guests sat there with mouths agape as if

awaiting the punchline. The other half craned their necks, unsure whom he meant.

Anne started to gesture with one hand but stopped. She started to say something, and failed. She cleared her throat.

Eric's heart thundered in his chest and he felt a tightness in his throat. He'd never cared as much about anything as he did about her answer.

Genevieve and Hainsworth Knox beamed at him as if they didn't mind in the least that he failed to marry their daughter. He noticed that they were holding hands on the table, in plain view. Had someone spiked their morning coffee?

Budge Bellamy seized upon the silence to renew his attack. "What do you mean, saying it's your wedding day if she'll have you? You don't just make an announcement like that, boy! You don't tell the world you're getting married until you've received the other party's permission!"

"Why not?" he said. "Caroline did."

"Come again?" In the middle of pouring himself a cup of coffee, his father forgot what he was doing and barely jerked his hand away in time to avoid a burn. A waiter rushed to clean the mess.

"What's this about your engagement?" Viv asked.

"Caroline announced it without consulting Eric," explained Lizzie, one of the few people with whom he'd shared this information. "She scheduled that big party last year on her own."

"That's not fair!" cried the loyal Petsy. "She isn't here to defend herself!"

"I think surprises are wonderful," gushed Saffron, the flaky minister, who was still hanging around.

This morning, she was decked out in a big white picture hat and a goofy, gauzy dress. "Surprise engagements, surprise weddings. It fits with the celestial energy flow, the nature of karma, of things meeting and parting and blending and separating."

"You sound like you're baking a cake!" harrumphed Petsy.

"I want to hear the truth from my son about his engagement," said Budge. "The one to Caroline Knox, not to this...this Crumm person."

"You can hear it from me instead!" Genevieve's commanding voice overrode even the boom of the Pretzel King. "My daughter admitted last night that she forced his hand. She manipulated him into agreeing to marry her."

"I could have said no," Eric pointed out.

"Why didn't you?" Kevin asked with cheerful curiosity as he began cleaning his third plate.

"It took me a long time, almost too long, to figure out what's important in life," he said. "I've loved Anne Crumm for five years but I never had the guts to admit it to myself. Well, I'm acknowledging it now. I love you, Anne, and I'll do anything you ask. Even if you tell me to go jump in the duck pond."

"Swans. Not ducks," said Joe. "Trust me. I've seen them up close and personal."

Anne got to her feet. From her flaming cheeks, Eric could tell he'd upset her. He wished he could take back that offer about jumping in the pond, because he suspected she was about to take him up on it.

ANNE HAD NO IDEA what she wanted to say. Public displays of emotion might suit the colorful Bellamys, but they were alien to her.

From the blur of faces, individuals came into focus. Lizzie, who'd given her the velvet dress. Hainsworth, brimming with fatherly affection. Genevieve's cousin from Texas, whose name escaped her, but who was nodding encouragement. They were all friends.

Over them towered Eric, his classically handsome face a study in fear and hope and love. He'd bared his soul, taking a big risk for her. Anne had to stop staring and give him an answer.

"Last night," she said, "you started to propose and I wouldn't let you."

Eric rubbed his chin ruefully. "You told me I needed to think it through."

"Now you're bringing it up again," she said. "The very next morning." Her voice rang through the small room and came back with a muffled echo.

"Yeah, it's true. I haven't really applied a lot of brainpower," Eric conceded.

Was he changing his mind? How dare he! "Do you mean it or not?"

He spread his arms. "Anne Crumm, I would follow you to the ends of the earth! I would even attend a publishers' party in New York with you, although I hope to high heaven you haven't planned any such boneheaded thing. Except for the one Caro made you organize, which is another story."

"I'm not following this," said Nana. "Does anybody know what he's talking about?"

"He's talking about the synthesis of two cardiopulmonary realities!" cried Saffron.

Anne saw that she'd better speak up before the rest

of the audience chose to express their opinions as
well. "Yes!" That didn't seem strong enough, so she
added, "I love you too, you byline thief, you ex-
ploiter of freelance writers, you spoiled hunk, you
wonderful crazy man!"

"Hey, it doesn't get much better than that!" declared Eric, and vaulted over a chair in his rush toward her.

An instant later his hands closed on Anne's waist
and she found herself lifted triumphantly above him.
Cheers greeted them; even Budge Bellamy smiled.

"Wed-ding! Wed-ding! Wed-ding!" chanted
Kevin. Winnie joined him, then Nana and, a moment
later, Vivian.

"Why not?" said Genevieve when Eric lowered
Anne to the floor. "We've got the minister, such as
she is, the food, the decorations and the assembled
guests, minus a few that nobody will miss."

"I vote yes!" Eric raised his hand. "Well, Anne?
You're the tiebreaker."

Objections thrummed in her mind: They didn't
have a ring. The paperwork couldn't be completed
until Monday. "My mother..." she began.

"We can get married again in California," Eric
volunteered. "Heck, we can get married as many
times as you like. The more married, the merrier."

She laughed. "Well, if you put it that way, who
am I to argue?"

The entire group joined the effort, lining up chairs
along an impromptu aisle and setting a spray of long-
stemmed roses in front of the buffet table to serve as
an altar. Lizzie wove some flowers together into a
lopsided bouquet. Although reluctant to admit she'd
held on to her wedding ring so long, Vivian produced

it from her purse and bestowed it upon her son as a gift to the happy couple.

Anne wasn't sure she wanted to celebrate this special occasion in a boring suit, even if she was wearing her best shoes. Before she could suggest retiring to change clothes, however, Nana wound a lavender scarf around her neck. Saffron graciously parted with her big white hat. From around her patrician neck, Genevieve removed an old-fashioned cameo and handed it to the bride.

"This is yours to keep," she said. "It's been mine since I was a girl. Neither of my daughters appreciate it, but I know you do."

Anne gave her a hug. "I consider you part of my family."

The older woman planted a kiss on her cheek. "And you're part of mine."

"I hope you'll include me in your family, too, Anne." Hainsworth offered his arm. "If you'll allow it, I'd like to give away the bride."

"I can't imagine anything I'd like better," she said.

The groomsmen lined up in their mismatched clothing. After the briefest of hesitations, Petsy joined the other bridesmaids, each carrying a rose plucked from one of the vases.

Eric took his place, broad-shouldered and radiating joy. If a few blades of grass clung to his loafers and the alligator embroidered on his polo shirt looked a trifle out of sorts, nobody seemed to care.

And so it came to pass that on June 20, in front of a well-filled buffet table, Eric Bellamy, son of the Pretzel King, did unite with Anne Crumm, heiress to nothing save an honest nature and a tart tongue.

Afterward, they ate a hearty repast. The cake was cut by Kevin Bellamy, who had grown tired of waiting for dessert.

"Wow," said Eric as he and Anne helped themselves to slices, "you can't beat this for convenience. Leftover flowers, leftover cake and a leftover groom."

"Leftover grooms are the very best kind," she said, and leaned closer for a kiss.

If you missed any of the two previous titles in
THE WEDDING PARTY, *you can still order
them from our Reader Service information at
the beginning of the book.*

782 LIZZIE'S LAST-CHANCE FIANCÉ
by Julie Kistler

786 RSVP...BABY
by Pamela Browning

*This holiday season, dash to
the delivery room with*

The McIntyre brothers of Bison City, Wyoming,
have no idea they're about to become daddies—
until a little stork tells them to hustle down to
the delivery room!

*Don't miss this exciting new series from three of
your favorite American Romance® authors!*

October 1999
BABY BY MIDNIGHT?
by Karen Toller Whittenburg (#794)

November 1999
COUNTDOWN TO BABY
by Muriel Jensen (#798)

December 1999
BABY 2000
by Judy Christenberry (#802)

Available wherever Harlequin books are sold.

HARLEQUIN®
Makes any time special™

Visit us at: www.romance.net

HARDELD

Looking For More Romance?

Visit Romance.net

Look us up on-line at: http://www.romance.net

Check in daily for these and other exciting features:

Hot off the press

View all current titles, and purchase them on-line.

What do the stars have in store for you?

Horoscope

Hot deals

Exclusive offers available only at Romance.net

Plus, don't miss our interactive quizzes, contests and bonus gifts.

PWEB

"Don't miss this, it's a keeper!"
—Muriel Jensen

"Entertaining, exciting and
utterly enticing!"
—Susan Mallery

"Engaging, sexy…a fun-filled romp."
—Vicki Lewis Thompson

See what all your favorite authors
are talking about.

Coming October 1999 to a retail store near you.

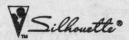

Look us up on-line at: http://www.romance.net   PHQ4992

In celebration of Harlequin®'s golden anniversary

Enter to win a *dream!* You could win:

- A luxurious trip for two to *The Renaissance Cottonwoods Resort* in Scottsdale, Arizona, or

- A bouquet of flowers once a week for a year from **FTD**, or

- A $500 shopping spree, or

- A fabulous bath & body gift basket, including **K-tel**'s *Candlelight and Romance* 5-CD set.

Look for **WIN A DREAM** flash on specially marked Harlequin® titles by Penny Jordan, Dallas Schulze, Anne Stuart and Kristine Rolofson in October 1999*.

RENAISSANCE.
COTTONWOODS RESORT
SCOTTSDALE, ARIZONA

*No purchase necessary—for contest details send a self-addressed envelope to Harlequin Makes Any Time Special Contest, P.O. Box 9069, Buffalo, NY, 14269-9069 (include contest name on self-addressed envelope). Contest ends December 31, 1999. Open to U.S. and Canadian residents who are 18 or over. Void where prohibited.

PHMATS-GR

HARLEQUIN®
AMERICAN ◆ ROMANCE®

COMING NEXT MONTH

#793 WILDCAT COWBOY by Cathy Gillen Thacker
The McCabes of Texas
Wade McCabe was not a Texan to be messed with. Only, nobody told
that to Josie Corbett, who was every bit his equal. And while Josie
wasn't looking to play a role in any McCabe baby-making scheme, she
did want to lasso wildcat Wade on her own terms. But there was no
resisting this Texas playboy—or his matchmaking family.

#794 BABY BY MIDNIGHT? by Karen Toller Whittenburg
Delivery Room Dads
Alex McIntyre knew Annie Thatcher was pregnant with *his* baby—but
the stubborn woman wouldn't admit it! Alex hadn't forgotten their
steamy night of passion—no way was Annie going to the
delivery room alone when Alex was right there, finally ready to be a
husband and daddy!

#795 THE VIRGIN & HER BODYGUARD by Mindy Neff
Tall, Dark & Irresistible
Raquel Santiago's small country home was not big enough for her, her
baby photography studio and one very brawny man. Babies to the left,
babies to the right and Cole Martinez covered in infant spit-up and
all-male sweat. He radiated strength and virility and gentleness that
Raquel could not resist. Cole was all too happy to indulge her
fantasies—except for his promise to her father....

#796 A MATCH MADE IN TEXAS by Tina Leonard
For a woman who had never known romance, Mary van Doorn was
getting a double helping from Jake Maddox. But with the responsibility
of six sisters and their sunflower farm, she was *not* shopping for a man.
The locals, though, had a different plan: one that would keep the
population of small-town Sunflower Junction, Texas, on the rise!

Look us up on-line at: http://www.romance.net

HARLEQUIN · CELEBRATES

FIVE DECADES OF ROMANCE

In October 1999,
Harlequin Intrigue®
delivers a month of our
best authors, best miniseries
and best romantic suspense
as we celebrate Harlequin's
50th Anniversary!

Look for these terrific
Harlequin Intrigue® books
at your favorite retail stores:

STOLEN MOMENTS (#533)
by B.J. Daniels

MIDNIGHT CALLER (#534)
by Rebecca York

HIS ONLY SON (#535)
by Kelsey Roberts

UNDERCOVER DAD (#536)
by Charlotte Douglas

Look us up on-line at: http://www.romance.net   H50I_L